I0726875

COST OF FREEDOM

TOKI MATSUDAIRA

WORKBOOK PRESS LLC
187 E Warm Springs Rd,
Suite B285, Las Vegas, NV 89119, USA

Website: https://workbookpress.com/
Hotline: 1-888-818-4856
Email: admin@workbookpress.com

Ordering Information:
Quantity sales. Special discounts are available on quantity purchases by corporations, associations, and others.
For details, contact the publisher at the address above.

Library of Congress Control Number:

ISBN-13:   978-1-960752-67-3 (Paperback Version)
              978-1-960752-68-0 (Digital Version)

REV. DATE: 22/07/2022

COST OF FREEDOM

TOKIKO MATSUDAIRA

CONTENTS

CHAPTER 1

DIVIDE WIND

In the year 1274 AD Japan was attacked by Mongolian forces and about to lose when a Divine Wind or major typhoon swept the country and forced the invading enemy to be swept away and die. This famous history in Japan first gave the extraordinary event another name called Kamikaze, which means Divine Wind. Eventually, when the tide turned against Japan in the Second World War, a last resort was called for. They asked for suicide pilots by the same name-Kamikaze or Divine Wind, to fly okha or baka bombs "crazy bombs." They were to fly straight into the enemy target and explode the bomb held in the plane on the targets of enemy ships and their fleet. There was to be no turning back for the Kamikaze pilots for they were Japan's heroes for the Imperial and military service of the Emperor. There were eventually to be few pilots left to serve out this terrible but very real command and this resulted in recruiting student boys. As the Divine Wind had invaded the Mongolian forces out of Japan in the 13th century, so Japan had hoped beyond hope for a miracle that would send away the allied forces moving closer and closer into Japanese waters and their territory. The lives claimed on both sides were high. It became a fact of daily routine to send off squadrons of youths employed as suicide bombers to attack the enemy by bombardment and by self-crashing , exploding like bombs in their nightmares of "baka" suicide deaths. This did not always put the youths who were elected to be the chosen suicide bombers at ease with their country or the cause so celebrated by Japanese war veterans of that time and later. Many poems and diaries have been published which can testify they did not wish to die at all, but resigned themselves to carrying out their suicidal task for their country and for the Emperor. For instance, on 11th May, Operation Kikusui No. 6 "At dawn, rain came. 40 army planes,26 Kemmu Squadron and Thunder Gods fighter bombers whose targets were American war ships off the East coast of Okinawa began their strikes at 5am. A Sub Lt. leader of the 10th Kemmu Squadron… boasted that he would "skim the surface of the sea and crash into the exact centre of his target and then cried out "Mother, the navy are trying to kill me!" His strange behavior was typical of the mixed emotions of the young Thunder Gods pilots."

On another occasion, a summary of a chat to his Kamikaze pilots went along these lines: he received the report of the Kamikaze attacks with tears in his eyes: "This was the summary of his last greeting to his young men : "You are already gods! Being gods, you must be beyond all desires…"

In a last resort battle for Iwo Jima, in 1945, when American traffic and artillery was heavier, an incident brought out these words from another pilot who said "it would be nothing more than a sacrifice." The war for Iwo Jima developed into a raging battle between the Americans and the Japanese which ended with the American Marines running to the summit of the hill where they hoisted the American flag. This was a clear statement recognizing victory in the battle for Iwo Jima. This was the turning point in the battles developing a new turn in the succeeding battles to follow for the Americans victory in the continuing war.

Often we hear of last ditch attempts, and the improbability of continuing to hold on to life for a moment longer. The days and nights of the Okha bombers who crash dived in "uncontrollable flying bombs" heard mutterings of the "terrible irresponsibility that he, too was silenced by the very magnanimous military service he had become engaged with." The Commander of the 5th Naval Aviation Fleet was Vice Admiral Ugaki. This was the man who would disobey orders to stop all attacks on all fronts. A courageous and brilliant fighter, close to the Imperial Court, he remained without doubt, one of the foremost leaders of the War one can remember by name. He will always remain in history as a loyal advocate for the Imperial High Command and close ally of all who served him. He encouraged his men to be brave in the face of battle without shedding a tear about it. He was enthusiastic to get on with "with the show" and never thought of battles as anything other than a fight against the enemy with a purpose to send volleys of strikes and more strikes until the enemy knew the meaning of the exercise. He was a favored man, amongst his team and his leadership gave him a record of brilliance in strategy and style of courageous and brave effort to the end. He was one who refused to obey the wishes and command of the High Command when told to cease all fire. He fought brilliantly to the very end. He survived the war and ended his career on foreign shores, as late as 2008!

One remembers that the Pacific War was not only a conflict between the Japanese and the Americans, It was a fight for South East Asia and naturally the Allies joined in the War, to secure defend various South East Asian countries such as Burma, Singapore, together with their allies as well as Australians and New Zealanders were the enemy who fought the Japanese by land sea and air.

The wars and battles fought were inconceivable for the Japanese, the cost of each battle ringing down further the economy of an already poverty stricken nation in a hair raising attempt to restore Japan back to the Empire they had known in an earlier time. The war established and fought for the ideal world of Empire for the greater Japan and it's sustained warfare in the battles that raged and became the historic legend favoring an all out win or loss for the holy war of a nation hoping for a recovery which could never be won even in the last resort. It has been said that had Japan entered the war soon, using Kamikaze suicide bombers, some allies believed at the time, that Japan would probably have won the war. The self crashing method was a brilliant strategy in their opinion, which could force devastation to any enemy no matter how superior their own defense might be. The psychological damage to their enemy could win rewards of a war to be won rather then the defeat they suffered having come into the war a little late in the date.

CHAPTER 2
THE TIDE THAT TURNED

Operation Heaven Sent was launched on 31ˢᵗ March, which was to be the last of the battles calling upon 3ʳᵈ and 5ᵗʰ Naval Aviation Fleets on Allied Troops, under the command of Vice Admiral Ugaki. He thought that the only way to stop the American forces and force delay in planning their imminent landing in Okinawa by using warships. He started shelling the island. The Thunder Gods were to prepare for a quick sortie after this. There were by now many pilots and naval personnel who doubted that the war should continue. There were increasing sentiments of despair. By 1ˢᵗ April, at about 8.30 in Okinawa time, the Japanese sortie of five planes proved to be a failure as the arrival of 16000 enemy American soldiers on shore was witnessed by the Japanese. This proved a failure for the Japanese side hoping to leave and dispatch for another destination. By 2ⁿᵈ April, Kemmu Squadron started up their launch in a twilight attack with 500 kgs bombs! On both raids, the Americans proved to be more powerful than the Japanese side. It became nothing more than true suicide destroy them, before they reached their target. For instance, out of 12 bombers, only 3 crash dived into American ships. Each had 200 bullets to use in self-defense. It was understood that their chances of winning a victory over the Americans was very dim, no matter how determined they were. They knew death awaited them. At this juncture,

the demoralized men felt their deaths would be meaningless even though they were caught up in the mystique of giving up their lives for their country and that the system that created the myth was an inner faith of their divinity. Communication had all but broken and pilots were losing contact making death amongst the Kamikaze pilots, the obvious end. The ace pilot also most renowned for his flying as the fighter for Japan was Genda. It is said that he was the man who thought of the last ditch attempts by self-crashing. He was also an ace pilot and a remarkably courageous man, inspired with a sense of obligation to recover Japan, setting out a plan to win a terrible war which would never be won by their side. He together with others agreed on the attack on Pearl Harbor. At a meeting amongst the seniority of Japan's military, it was confirmed that the new air corps would be called Kamikaze or "Divine Wind" or the Kamikaze Special Attack Corps. This was top secret and confidential only to those who participated in the meeting that took place. The Americans always knew that had the Japanese entered the war sooner, they might have stood a chance better to winning it. The force and strength of the Americans seen with their battalions of ships and bombers could never be matched by the Thunder Gods whose invasions against their forces proved their strength with their unbelievable build up of ships, bombers and heavy artillery. There was little indication that their raids had reduced the numbers of US ships cruising in the area. The kamikaze Special Attack Corps was to be divided into four units-Shikishima, Yamato, Asahi and Namazakura. Hardly could their self-sacrifice and surrender of their own lives be better rewarded than to secure it all for a better future .Japan's war with Kamikaze pilots was to become the mystique and the essential cause celebrated of this ferocious war. The first sortie of the sure-death units – the Yamato in Cebu, the Shikishima, Asahi, and Yamazakura at Mobalacat was postponed due to bad weather. The same night, 300 conventional aircraft of the 2nd Naval Aviation Fleet "carried out" systematic attacks and "raids" against the American fleet. This was successful but the results minimal. One aircraft carrier and 2 cruisers, 3 destroyers had been sunk. A Kamikaze pilot had to fly okha carrying under it a Betty to drop it in the area which had been targeted. In a touching episode of great dignity before retiring for the night, one of the young fighter pilots pulled out his notebook and wrote on the back cover "After some 20 years, I have nothing to leave behind, except this little notebook, which I dedicate to my parents, who have always enfolded me in love. " They clearly did not long for their premature deaths to come. In another instance, another flight pilot did not want to give the training show, scheduled to be tested for the Admiral who was about to arrive. The point was that he was ready to leave on a real war mission in the Okha, but felt a demonstration and show in live action for the Admiral to watch was unnecessary. Understanding his feelings, the camp corps administrator explained this and relieved the young pilot from the pageantry that had been arranged for the Admiral who was waiting to see the show. "There is no need to practice this training schedule" he said to the young Thunder God and went and cancelled it. The uniform or wear of the Okha pilots was a short sword and a white headband with Thunder Gods written in "large red characters."

The Americans were wealthy and could afford more sophisticated planes boats and artillery. It is true to say that the Japanese side was not short of extremely good pilots, courageous to the end. They never out measured or make inferior those fighting the Americans during that war. For Japan, it was the wind of divine self-sacrifice for a holy war for like the petals of the falling cherry blossoms, the young soldiers fell in their last ditch attempts to secure a war against the strength of the American forces. Hard and bitter battles ensued with an unbelievable build up of heavy artillery that Thunder Gods would never match. Although the American fleet could re-capture the Philippines through technical superiority, it was to be a test of enormous consequence that would lead to the destruction of the three rings protecting that fleet. Meanwhile, Japanese sentiment against the Imperial military sending them all to terrifying and suicidal war led one of the officers to believe it was impossible to prevent suicide missions for suicide attacks by the Emperor's military forces. He knew the Imperial system was absolute. His own brother who had revolted against the system, had sacrificed his life in the attempt. The Thunder Gods and their officers were caught up in a dilemma- they were forced to obey any order they were given. It was imminent that Thunder Gods ultimately died in exploding cherry blossom attacks of which 49 crew members of Betty mother planes gave their lives. 172 fighting Thunder Gods were killed during this period. Officers too fell. The reminder of America's rule over the Pacific made the mood of the men, morbid and despondent. Toward the end of the war, in 1945, a series of operations of suicide pilots calling themselves "exploding cherry blossom" took place, and various attacks followed. Squadrons dis-appeared. Many died. Altogether 172 men, including fighter bombers pilots assigned to the Thunder Gods corps, were killed during this period. 70 men were left in the corps composed of 2 division leaders, 5 reserve officers and 63 petty officer pilots. The courage to follow showed Operation Kikusui no. 2, "all out running attack against the enemy, Task Force". It was a game of ten little Indians, when one moved over, and left nine…It was –"until tomorrow, when the no 5 man left them with only 4 men left behind. Stored wooden boxes containing private articles of the Thunder Gods who had already died were kept safely to be returned to their families.

The responsibility remained with the living comrades and fellow pilots. The daily occurrence of death passed by solemnly. They promised one thing to each other. "We'll all meet at Yasukuni Shrine". This is a shrine in Tokyo for the dead war heroes. The Japanese realized that the American invasion fleet used techniques developed in the re-capture of the Philippines. The three rings that protected their defense were perfect and almost impenetrable. A secondary ring made up of picket line or radar patrol ships circled by destroyers and other vessels. The third was a wall of anti-aircraft guns on warships guarding the carriers and troop ships. The Japanese side had to meet these challenges. They must force the enemy off their shores and save their country like the original Kamikaze in the 13th century.

The air corps had evacuated to Shokoku, northern Kyushu and was ordered to return immediately to Southern Khyushu and was ordered back to headquarters of the Thunder Gods. The Thunder Gods were ordered to protect the Miyazaki area. Okamura, Iwaki, Seki and other officers in the corps moved from Kanoya to Tomitaka, where three fighter squadrons were waiting. They knew "they could not just stand by in the midst of the coming calamity. Decisive battles for Iwo Jima took place at 3pm February 17th in "the fiercest battles of the Pacific". The American marines "stormed" and "took the island". It didn't take long before Yokohama-Tokyo areas came under American attack by their bombers. This was the beginning of many air raids on Tokyo and it's surroundings. This was the former capital of the Samurai Shogunate, where the Imperial Palace stood with their Imperial presence. They took care not to bomb this architectural masterpiece and other cites of importance both in Tokyo and in other areas of Japan for the sake of respect and obligation to Japan's cultural and integral national heritage.

This was the beginning of many air raids in both Tokyo and other surrounding areas. Some attacks included as many as 200 planes, enough to dysfunction entire cities. Kyushu and Honshu, were attacked as a daily occurrence and American submarines haunted the shores of Kyushu Islands. Full scale attack on the main island was endless. Taiwan was cut off and air bases for Thunder God missions were often abandoned against the allied forces. The wealthy American bombers started their invasion of Okinawa against 5th Naval Aviation seeking shelter in dimly lit and small bunkers. The evidence proved the superiority of American fighters over Okinawa Island, knocking out in one morning, airfields and destroying many ships. Thunder Gods base Miyazaki Air Base was raided by the American bombers targeting Kyushu and Kagoshima Prefecture.

The force and the strength of the Americans were seen in their ships and bombers with heavier artillery and unbelievable build-up which could not be matched by the Thunder Gods. It was a case of all or nothing for the Kamikaze pilots by now. There was no indication that their raids had reduced the number of U.S. ships in that area. Operation Kikusui No 1was another last ditch series of aerial attacks against the Allied Forces. Battleship "Yamato" was sent to Okinawa where its huge guns could wreck havoc among the American ships. Admiral Toyoda had launched the Yamato together with 8 destroyers to leave and head back for Okinawa. The objective was to destroy totally the support ships, aircraft carriers as well as battle ships and to capture and annihilate enemy landing forces. Instead, the great warship was pounded on all sides by every conceivable flying boats-torpedoes and bombing runs fired time and time again. Its vessels had been hit by six bombs and ten torpedoes. The world's largest battleship finally exploded and sank without ever having engaged once in a naval battle. This was yet again a "devastating blow to Japan." 5th April, Operation Kikusui was about to be launched when the Koiso Cabinet resigned en bloc, and the 79 year old retired Naval Admiral Kantaro Suzuki, was appointed Prime Minister. Suzuki had been the grand Chamberlain and Privy Councilor at the time of the infamous February 26th incident in 1936, when a group of rebellious officers including the brother of one of the squadron leaders, had staged an unsuccessful coup against the government, killing several high ranking officials and wounding Suzuki and others. Meanwhile the Emperor's stand to end the war was a reason that Suzuki was appointed the Minister he could trust to carry out his bidding. He strongly supported the last-ditch stand against the Allied Forces in Okinawa. At the same time, he knew he could probably be assassinated by military extremists immediately thereafter. However, in spite of the gamble, he realized as well that the outcome of that battle would determine his chances to end the war anytime very soon.

At 12.30, Japanese planes met the first ring of American fighter planes. Several Japanese aircraft shot before the main fore broke through and proceeded to Okinawa,

"The second ring and the picket line of American radar patrol vessels, succeeded in blowing up Japanese planes out of the air". However more than half of the Japanese aircraft survived the American defensive ring, and began their final approach to Okinawa." Vice Admiral Ugaki responsible for the strategies held in the counter attack plan told them to hurry and quicken their preparations." The Thunder Gods and the army and navy pilots in Taiwan were to attack in a series of joint suicide missions. Vice Admiral Ugaki, realized the last big gamble, being the main targets of the Thunder Gods corps, were to be the American warships anchored in Okinawa. The mission was to be for the Okha exploding cherry blossoms to chase after aircraft carriers and other warships cruising in the vicinity.

The American ships in the vicinity lay in "smoke screens peppering the sky with anti-aircraft barrages. Those that were anchored in harbors joined in anti-aircraft guns. The ensuing battle became a nightmare of exploding planes and ships, with smoke fireballs, and metallic debris filling the air... Despite the defensive maneuvers of the American ships, several dozen Thunder Gods and other suicide pilots managed to hit their targets setting some of them ablaze and sending others to the bottom in a matter of minutes."

"Mayday, mayday signals were sent as the barrage of heavy attacks continued." After the carnage was over, two American destroyers, minesweepers and two ammunition carriers had been sunk. Ten destroyers, one destroyer escort, one light carrier, several minesweepers and a number of other American vessels had been badly damaged. Vice Admiral Ugaki then sent a coded telegram to Admiral Toyoda: "It now seems advisable to overcome all our difficulties and mount an all out offensive against the enemy. Utmost efforts are now being made to round up the necessary materials and planes to continue special suicide attacks." Toyoda wrote back agreeing in his reply: "There is every indication that the enemy's forces have been thrown into disarray providing a delicate war opportunity."

On 8th April, military headquarters in Tokyo announced that in the past three days, Japanese aerial forces had sunk two special aircraft carriers, one battleship, one destroyer, five troop transport ships and six unidentified vessels, and as well put three additional battleships, three cruisers, seven transport ships, six other unidentified vessels out of communication. They learned they had sunk three destroyers, three other vessels, two air-craft carriers, one battleship, twenty-one cruisers, and seven other ships. The success of Operation Kikusui No 1 under Vice Admiral Ugaki was an agreeable change from the previous attacks on the Yamato.

9th April, Admiral Ugaki gave over the order for an immediate launch of Operation Kikusui No 2!

April 11th, the day the rain stopped. 60 navy planes, including 16 Thunder Gods Fighter bombers from the 5th Kemmu Squadron, attacked American ships in Kikaigashima Island. 3 Thunder Gods were unable to reach their target and returned to air base.

12 April-the day of Doha's raid. A sortie was led with the remaining okha pilots in their move from Tomitaka in Kanoya Base. There were now 70 men left in the corps-two division leaders, 5 reserve officers and 63 petty officer pilots. Recruits were ordered to be assigned to the Thunder Gods corps , including the Tornado corps at Konoike Base. The follow up to the Operation Kikusui No 2 was "All out Running Attacks Against the Enemy Task Force". Thunder God pilots selected for the first attack were posted resolved to fight to the end.

14 April dawned bright and clear. A daylight attack was imminent. Seven okha planes, the sixth Kemmu Squadron, and two squadrons of Thunder Gods fighter-bombers (laden with 250 kg bombs) took off and headed for a fleet of American aircraft carriers that had been sighted some 85 miles east of some Japanese territorial Islands. 125 fighter planes had been gathered from various air bases to provide cover for the suicide attack against the American ships. In the meanwhile, Captain Minoru Genda had been transferred from the naval General Staff.

These pilots remembered and known as special attack forces , human missiles, god-like soldiers, "blossoms in the wind" and countless other slogans of heroism. They cast such terror and fear to many Americans and allies who lost their reserve and developed war traumas which had not expressed itself until the last years of the desperate struggle in the war. The last battles fought between the Japanese and the Americans for the homeland, at its worst in the pitched battles for Okinawa finished the Thunder Gods corps. On 8th June, 1945 the American war planes raided dozens of targets in Kyushu, including Japanese air bases, where several planes were set afire and 40 others damaged.

The battles that ensued for Okinawa lasted from April through June. There were altogether ten sorties and Operation Kikusui. Many among the Thunder Gods were getting demoralized by the hapless way the war was going and they went about their duties with less and less enthusiasm. There was growing demoralization. It's side effects showed terrible strains on the troops. A growing problem of keeping the corps together developed as the days ran into months. By 8th June, 270 war planes raided dozens of targets in Kyushu, including Japanese held air bases of important military location, where several planes were set on fire and others damaged. By the 9th Operation Kikusui the Americans were launching attacks on the Japanese mainland, though Okinawa was still held by the Japanese fleets where constant bombardment and attacks were suffered by both sides.

After the appeal of the "Mayday, Mayday" call by the American ships staggered back to Hawaii. Admiral Halsey replaced the former American Admiral, who exercised "show off" flights over Kyushu to menace the Japanese side with their effects.

The leisurely attacks and manner of the planes which took off served a purpose against the Japanese who never left the defense of the islands. Although Vice Admiral Ugaki never lost sight of his commitment to the war, he struck the American naval forces by launching an attack using Thunder Gods. This was to force the Americans to retreat from Okinawa Leyte Gulf, ending their support of the Okinawa invasion.

The Americans drove a hard battle in the last of the 32nd Army Corps from "the ruins of a Castle along the mainland of Okinawa, and though a squadron was dispatched by the Japanese side to attack the American corps, they were never heard of or seen again, having disappeared completely. Such incidents occurred regularly during this near end of war before the declaration of defeat and surrender came about.

Although a major Operation Ketsugo (Last Resort) was to be launched staging an all out suicide attack against the enemy, this could not be carried out as the okha type -22 bomb failed the test and a new project had to be planned.

The battles for Okinawa was lost. Kikusui Operations were suspended after the completion of Operation No 10. This final sortie was a complete failure. On the same day, 32nd Army Corps men started killing themselves. At dawn on 23 June, Commander Mitsuri Ushigima and Chief of Staff Isamu Cho committed hara kiri. The battle for Okinawa was over.

FINAL

Because of the Thunder Gods Corps, and special suicide missions sent to attack American military in the Pacific, at the turn of the war, the Americans gave vent to their views about the torment caused by the Japanese side. On 10th August, approximately 3.30pm, an air raid took place in Hiroshima. This announcement came directly from the military headquarters. In the midst of all the confusion and communication levels at their most pitiful, the announcement said that a small number of B-29 bombers had raided Hiroshima and that a new type of bomb had exploded causing severe damage. The incident was being investigated. Another message reported that a new bomb might have been an A-bomb, but no one believed such a weapon would materialize during the war. In fact little information was affordable or available for the sake of a nation who had just been devastated at the war's end by a disadvantage and disability such as would happen at the end of any World War. The Americans had sent an atomic bomb to Hiroshima, to make things a little worse for Japan just at the stage of the war's end. This was not information available to the poor Japanese.

9th June, Russian troops cross the border into Manchuria in a surprise attack on Japan.

10th August, at 11 am a second A-bomb was dropped on Nagasaki.

Americans started shelling Tokyo-Yokohama area and Vice Admiral Ugaki who had by now been appointed Commander-in-chief of the Combined Naval Aviation Fleet, recognized the shelling as the beginning of the enemy's planned invasion on the homeland.

11th August, he received instructions from the Navy General Headquarters to launch an attack against American ships off the main island of Honshu as well as against those still berthed at Okinawa. Ugaki ordered six planes from the Thunder Gods Corps fighter bombers laden with 500 kg bombs, to stand by on Kikaigashima Island, to carry out strikes against US ships in Okinawa ports. That afternoon, Ugaki received a copy of a message broadcast by San Francisco radio that Japan must surrender on condition that the Emperor be retained.

The Potsdam Declaration would be written engaging in a self styled peace treaty, eventually, by the initiation of their San Francisco radio.

12th August, Radio San Francisco predictably sees how the Allies could not accept Japan's demand that the Imperial system be preserved as a condition of surrender. He hoped to quash the plot (Ugaki) to surrender Japan to the enemy.

The brave Ugaki suspected however that the movement might have just been a trade exercise to test out and "see" how the Americans would react. He continued preparations for the last ditch defense of his country.

13 August, Japan was urged to surrender to avoid more bloodshed and destruction, but Ugaki, ignored them. He was obsessed to defend Japan to the death while waiting for Vice Admiral RYONUSUKE KUSAKA, who had been delayed in arriving to take over from Vice Admiral Ugaki.

That same day, five Thunder Gods fighter bombers took off from Kikaigashima Island, headed for Okinawa.

At 6.50p.m, radio messages came in from the two other planes that had continued toward Okinawa. They radioed that they were making their dives.

However, no more missions by the Thunder Gods Corps were to be.

14th August, news about Japan's defeat and imminent surrender became more specific. It was reported that General Douglas MacArthur, Supreme Commander of the Allied Forces was soon arriving in Tokyo. Ugaki accepted the idea that Japan's surrender had been arranged without anyone having consulted him even once.

At 10.30am, 200 B-29 bombers could be seen from Ugaki's headquarters, flying northward. Bombings took place at Iwakuri Air Base and other targets in that vicinity. Enemy landing was at hand and putting the entire country on alert. Ugaki did not believe the enemy was about to invade the country. He thought they were trying to intimidate and force Japan's surrender.

Just before midnight, on August 14th, he received the order to cease all hostile action against American forces in Okinawa and against

Soviet forces in Manchuria.

The Potsdam Declaration declared that war criminals would be severely punished. What was meant by "war criminals" was not well taken or understood.

The Emperor's address to end the war was not well accepted by many in the Japanese military .Many of them did not or could not accept this state of affairs, and deliberately disobeyed orders and kept up action to serve hostility. No consensus could be reached about ending the war. Meetings took place on 14 August. The Emperor stepped into this and decided that the war should be concluded immediately. Still unable to accept this decision, many of the soldiers shouted: "Continue the war! The decisive battle should be on Japan proper".

CONCLUSION

The Japanese could never match their strength. The Japanese felt they must do their last resort to the end and to the death. In a movie I saw as a student ,a Japanese naval officer who had studied at a University in the United States was quoted as saying that after Pearl Harbor "The American was like a sleeping giant and when awakened, would have a terrible resolve."11am 10th August, a second A-bomb was dropped on Nagasaki.

Nobody thought the nuclear weapon would be used though there had been speculation about this happening for sometime. Certainly their purity of spirit for a greater Japan whose future lay with the children they left behind holding their promise to them for a finer and brighter day would one day come true. The eventual economic recovery and miracle for that final end so difficult to imagine after the humiliating post surrender would once again come true as the blossoms in the petals of the tiny pink cherry blossoms would return at the approach of each spring. The nation that had lost the Pacific War, would meet a man representing the side who conquered and who would open the door for the miracle that was about to happen when they sent their General Douglas MacArthur , the Supreme Commander-in-Chief of the Allied Forces in the Pacific, whose sympathy for the Emperor, gave Japan that hope for the recovery sought and fought in the hopeless battles of Last Resorts, the human sacrifices not overlooked by the means of suicide bombers and Thunder Gods. The wild promise made by each kamikaze pilot suddenly appeared in the distant horizon as the way would be assured for peace and stability in a nation torn by a terrible war. All they had fought so hard for was about to happen. They realized that through defeat, the dream of the empires of wealth that had been their past history, and which many had died for, would not get lost in that final and unforgettable war of the Pacific.

The cherry blossom comes out in the spring, small pink blossoms on a tree. They were to represent the symbol of spring as "Okha" or "exploding cherry blossoms" which must fall and die. They are the symbol of a promise and hope. It is the period before the high summer when the amazing heat of the sun would drive the people to the shores or to the mountains. It is a tradition in Japan to celebrate the springtime of early summer when the cherry blossom returns. It is also a reminder of the Thunder Gods and the last Great War when many perished like "fallen cherry blossoms."

Although many former kamikaze pilots who lived and survived, felt remorse and despondency afterward, in a postwar Japan that to any would be a reality of ruin and diminished poverty so extreme that there was hardly any food, and people in the streets were more than begging to stay alive. They often traded in their clothes in exchange for food, and ended up in rags. There was rampant illness such as cholera. Many died. It was a ravaged nation with no government and no sense of awareness anymore. It would take a lot to bring it back to normality and essence. Even a war baby had little chance to survive with the air raids and bombings going on in Tokyo, especially. The war had cost the lives of most of their bravest men and sons. Mothers might live to tell if lucky enough to survive the post surrender era of a defeated Japan from 1945.

The Patriots shrine

The Japanese acronym on an inscription in a popular Buddhist prayer went along these lines, calling itself Hi-Ri-Ho-Ken-ten: Irrationality can never match reason, reason can never match law-law can never match power-power can never match heaven. This well known line is synonymous to the philosophy and thinking of Japanese scholars. It bears a light on another" frame of mind" which is oriental not western in perception. I hazard a guess to say that as east and west do meet more frequently now, that such well known acronyms is not foreign or unusual to the more discerning person whose sympathy reaches out to

Japan.

Post surrender Japan 1945-1947"The Potsdam Proclamation declared the Japanese nation would not be enslaved or destroyed as a nation, but would lose their Empire. While under surrender, the country would be under military occupation and "stern justice" would be given to "war criminals." The authority and influence of those who had "deceived and misled the people of Japan into World War 11 conquest would be exacted and eliminated for all time "just reparation in kind" would be exacted, military forces would be completely disarmed ,the economy would be demilitarized but eventually permitted to return to world trade: and the government would be required to remove all articles to the revival and strengthening of democratic tendencies among the "Japanese people." Establishing freedom of speech, religions, thought, as well as respect of fundamental human rights. The Occupation would be terminated when there "had been established in accordance with the freely expressed will of the Japanese people a peacefully inclined and responsible government..."

The Potsdam Policy

1.To insure that Japan will never again become a menace to the United States or to the peace and security of the world.

2. To bring about the eventual establishment of a peaceful and responsible government which will respect the rights of other states and will support the objectives of the United States as reflected in the ideals and principles of the United Nations. The U.S. desire that this government should conform as closely as may be to principles of democratic self-government but it is not the responsibility of the allied powers to impose upon Japan any form of government not supported by the freely expressed will of the people.

It was for the remaking political, social, cultural and economic fabric of a defeated nation, and in the process change their way of thinking. This was most helpful to both sides and at the same time constructive. The conquerors were defining "their grand missions as they went along."

While Germany was drafting post surrender policy, all of Japan was placed under American control. Occupied Germany however was divided into U.S., British, French and Soviet zones and at the same time there was East and West Germany.

Political Japanese prisoners were released after 18 years in prison. They were Communists!

Shidehara Kijime was appointed the new President of Japan, who met McArthur who told him that he wanted "liberalization "of the constitution. The Government had many things to re-organise such as giving liberal education, democratic economy and to "revise" monopolies of industrial control" and in general promote labor unions and allow greater equality to women, which would generally eliminate "despotic vestiges in society." This was his project as dated October 11, 1945.

The government wanted antimonopoly system to replace the monopoly of rural landlord class, whose former exploitative tenancy was as unfair and unpopular as the new way was popular and accepted. The small owner farmers of property could be free to work without the restraint and imposition of the previous policy. They also insisted on the centralization of a more democratic government rather than the older and more feudalistic systems set up before the war. This included giving women the right to vote. Both were passed through legislation and accepted by the government as the policy to follow." War criminals" class A were accused and on the whole executed if they had not already committed suicide.

Government sponsored cult of the Shinto was abolished on 15 December.

The elimination of the feudalist and military system was renounced. This had been observed as the great cause of the war . Thus, the way was paved for the pacifist course.

Eventually by the right for women to vote, conforming policing and otherwise submitting a law governing working condition, as well as revising the education system and renewing electoral systems by promotion of autonomy viz–a viz a central government's enduring act of democratic revolution, enabled the Emperor's subjects to become rightful citizens apart or away from the "traditional ways" which had to be stamped out.

I mention too at this stage that the war started in Manchuria for it's conquest by the Japanese forces as early as 1931. This gave prominence to blame Japan in the early days of the war which exploded into WW11

.All out war evolved against all of China in 1937. I will talk of this in later chapters. "

Post surrender

These were the years of Japan's woes. They were starving masses suffering "food rationing" often not delivered or not sent on time. There was insufficient food." Kyodatsu" was the main state of condition and the livelihood of the Japanese deteriorated into illness such as dysentery, cholera, typhoid, and tuberculosis. Many if not most of Japan was suffering this immediate condition just after the surrender of war. Often they starved and died in scores running into several hundred thousands! Consequently there was a lot of black market traffic where the poor sold their clothing in exchange for food. It was a hopeless situation with no end to keeping themselves barely alive. The children who understand often better than their parents held plays which seemed to involve finding pleasure in being colonized. They played being GI and prostitute. They play acted pimps earning money by introducing women to the GI's, the new conquerors of Japan! "You like to meet my sister?" became the same, as far as speaking English went, like saying "give me chocolate. "The child play by 1949 continued on as they portrayed being the unemployed vagrant. Crime was re-enacted in "dorabo gekko" or "catch a thief" instead of hide and seek. They played at "kaidashi-gekko" pretending to leave home to look for food. Post War Japan and the crisis proved to be a part of the "corruption and economic sabotage "against both Americans and Japanese .The post surrender time was notorious for the epidemic of crime that swept Japan due to an impoverishment and suffering newly found and full of poor people who were unable to have a glimpse of the promise made by the Occupation and their forces. They had been promised that Japan was to be led out of their destabilization and become once more a better off country amongst the world at large. Petty crime was rampant.

It was a time of opportunism and exploitation and even the judicial system waged war on the penniless and petty criminals, putting thousands into prisons. The exploiters and opportunists were people from the "former military, corrupt politicians and powerful gang leaders who did all but manipulate the systems for their own betterment and selfish pride." Anything good, had to come from the black market. Everybody went to the black market at least once, if not a lot of times.

Earlier the "Tokkotai" or more popular Kamikaze pilots turned to robbery. Tokkotai Kuzure or "degenerate Tokkotai" were destructive, drinking, womanizing criminals. The world had quickly changed and become one of turmoil and strife .The Tokkotai had turned to becoming known gangsters who accosted pedestrians in full daylight in the street and committed armed robberies. Even by 1950, "Kyodatsu " continued and the Japanese thought of themselves as a race who must "endure the unendurable" due to the long years of American occupation for finding a resolve to self govern and self help to get back in the main.

At this time, there were many writers and one especially comes to mind by the name of Horigucho Daigaku. He conveyed his own feelings about "transcending exhaustion and despair. "Culture was changing and often written about and he speaks of "love both carnal and pure." These were days of decadence and his poems declared the "provocative challenge to old orthodoxies."

Social life and society changed and a sense of release was felt away from the former old and rigidly controlled feelings of the years before. There was a sudden wave of light heartedness even amongst the hierarchy. Though some resigned themselves to serving their enemy but also the "conqueror", it also led many astray into the fields of prostitution where they met up with "women of the dark " in the parks. There were many who tried finding jobs but prostitution was the easiest way of finding money. When discovered they were rejected and forced back to Ueno Station. The Finance Minister Ikeda Hayaro, served his government by backing an arrangement saying "a hundred million yen is cheap for protecting chastity". Grateful, the entrepreneurs who served the nation in front of the Imperial palace shouted "Long Live the Emperor."

They enlisted protecting the "good" women of Japan, a well established policy in dealing with Western barbarians. Special pleasure quarters had been set up after the 19th Century when forcing the country to come out of seclusion in an effort to trade better. Mythology states Okichi was chosen and assigned as a consort for Townend Harris, 1st American Consul, who…the procurers of 1945 appropriated" her sad sensual image" when defining her task. The women assembled would be "showa no Tojin Okichi"…the Okichis of the present era.

"The watertrade" was an assignment to "stave and hold back the raging waves and defend and nurture the purity of our race…

"Tokyo R.A.A."paid homage and maintained as a national policy, a protectionism for the pure blood of the hundred million.""Pan Pan" openly prostituted themselves to the conqueror-while the "good" Japanese who consorted with the Americans as privileged elite, only did it figuratively.

Some women lost their chastity just for a pair of stockings. I think this was wide spread during the time of the War and after, whether it happened in Japan or in Europe. Good clothes were scarce and also very expensive. Food was rationed, and in many countries such as Germany, there was wide spread want. The relationship of women by those conquerors made forced slaves of sexual burden. Such is the obvious notoriety of being amongst the conquered. This led one to believe in the obvious water trade which was not to be treated like a threat but must be made to appear available to the conqueror! In a book, an author writes how "this characteristic colonial attitude led to a notorious incident in which all the women on a commuter train were detained by American MPs and forced to submit to medical examinations for venereal disease. Every Japanese woman, in a word, was potentially a whore." This further explains how the nation changed from one fit for an nihilism into a race worth more than an object receiving affection or respect and love. "The Pan Pan changed the course" and made it into a "delightful relationship of interracial affection" and it is agreed that "an important cultural event "was in fact taking place.

"In the words of a former military officer who wrote "I drank, trying to forget a life that hung suspended like a floating weed." They were the fallen who had aspired to die for their country −to fall with the purity and beauty of the cherry blossom as the mesmerizing cliché of the war years… were now robbing their countrymen. They knew survival was necessary in order to remember their promise of a rebuilding of their country and in that moment of promise before the War's end, they had cut out for themselves all the dreams that might one day come true. However, at this moment in time, they lived a dream of surviving in the joints of a dark market offering them all that could matter in days and nights of the deepest trouble. "All was irrelevant to the dark faces gathered in the black market.

Although life seemed to be endless gloom and unsettledness with renunciations on most people's mind, trying to survive day by day, night by night, one remembers the writers of the day whose forthright scripts have established another understanding of the thoughts in word deed and mind of the people living at the time.

A writer of the day called Sakaguchi (1946) is acclaimed for his work on Decadence which expressed his criticism of the war time experience. He cites the war and post war as a time of "human fraility and loneliness decaying in front of the world and society." Traditional values were thrown in the air that had always been the keep sake of the Japanese nation during the War. He wrote " the look of the nation since defeat is one of pure and simple decadence." Could anybody say that kamikaze was only an illusion and that human history begins from the point where he takes to black marketeering? The samurai spirit had lost it's allure and Japan might perish under the insignia of their decadent ways and life as it had now become. The esteem of the war had vanished into thin air and the call for a greater Japan was not in the horizon as far as the eye could see. Japan had plundered into a hopeless oblivion, and along this line they must pass in order to one day catch a glimpse of the dream created in the war for a better Japan. The spirit of the samurai, though not heard or seen, must one day return to lead the nation back into harmony with itself. So far, it was all but decadence and a society full of sickness and immorality.

Another writer known at the time for her involvement in the war in China, never forgot the horrors of the nation at war. She remember the "holy war" well.." .She was Tamura Tajira One writer, who will be remembered for his "angelic prose" was Dazai Osamu whose "kyodatsu condition" known in his novel "The Setting Sun" laments the meaning of noblesse oblige, which in turn, professes an understanding and philosophy of "love and resolution." He was an intelligent and somewhat outspoken man who wrote like an angel. He was also an alcoholic and drug addict even before the war, and though he committed suicide by jumping off a reservoir together with his girlfriend, his writings held such belief by many if not most, that he automatically became a legend of his time. Although like many writers, he was a Marxist, he never forgot his finer feelings which he expressed with great dignity. I will give you an example of his writing." We say defeated, defeated, but I don't think that's so. We've been ruined. Destroyed. (From one corner to the other, the country of Japan is being occupied, and every single one of us is a captive). Rural people who don't find this shameful are fools." In another anti-American short poem, he wrote this:

Not you,

Not you,

It was not you

We were waiting for."

He eventually wrote his great piece called "The Setting Sun", in which the heroine, Kazuko established a revolutionary love in defiance of the old traditional values and has an affair with an older man and an alcoholic, and carries and delivers his child. Although the mundane prospect of looking after the child is raised on an overwhelming scale of some deliberation, the matter of the story is her acceptance that the moral revolution conceived the child and she must raise the illegitimate child whose father is nothing better than an old man and a drunk. The little suicidal brother is a "little victim" of life. Not only this, but the emphasis employs the reality of the elderly drunken lover who has the" face of a victim" and that the "noble victim must be herself completely wasted in a lonely effort to staying alive." It is said "in her final letter to her alcoholic lover she equates victimization with beauty."

Kazai stresses how one falls victim to "causes greater than oneself." In his novel, he does unfold a new line and image of the "old" and of the "new" Japan. This leads to an understanding of the tortured course of the changes of life's way, with twists and turns connecting it up to a momentum of a new era, unfolding another meaning so far away from the "old morality". Though one, amongst writers of "flesh novels" he was" well born, well educated but considered a degenerate prone to self annihilation through self-indulgence". He appears to have applied himself to the" mystique "of the self destructive artist. In his book "Shayo" or "The Setting Sun" he applies his philosophy and creed to "love and revolution." About a year later, in a drunken state, he is discovered lying in the reservoirs with his mistress having killed himself.

The feudal Japan's strict distinction between love and marriage was that "good" women were taught they were inferior to women having to serve them (three generations of father, husband and son). They were taught that men might indulge in exotic love making, such pleasures and behavior were improper for a well bred woman. This was the role of "modern" married couples. Therefore the woman's destiny was considered to be "ryosai kenbo"-a good wife and wise mother. For example, her duty was to serve the male dominated family as the dutiful wife serving the imperial state.

"Fifu Seikatsu" was similar to the American periodical of that time. Sexology was the idiom causing the writer to discuss fundamental values of the meaning of the patriarchal family system and the family state which must return to it's natural destiny in society. The old ideologies regarding reciprocated love and sexual relationships between husband and wife must remain essential in order to keep a happy family unity without necessarily undermining the old ideologies of the Japanese past. Although much was changing in Japan after the War the changes only reinforced the traditional values of Japanese culture with new beliefs of communication away from the degeneracy that had built up over the years during and immediately after the War. Modernizing Japanese thinking was accepted for the sake of improving old standards and culture. It was to change from the old feudal system to a technocratic and a more superior state than before. This was disclosed as a medical problem. As the author, John Dower says and here I quote: "At the time of Post War Japan, lightheartedness flourished bringing a brighter and lighter hope for a future. Radio came back bringing with it a wave of new American style programs. Politics was made to appear funnier than before and the lighthearted trend gave forth a release from the old image of Japan and it's somewhat constrained ideologies and beliefs that were difficult for most to uphold, now, after such a devastating defeat. There was no more the familiar ring of putting up with it for pain or burden oneself in a drive of "weeping and gnashing of teeth." This transition was one from war to peace."

CHAPTER 3
THE BEGINNING OF TRADE

The economy was at its lowest ebb with so much black marketeering to sweep the nation on a course to live by the creeds offered by gangsters. So to work, they set themselves on to employ engaging better deals between the foreign military and the nationals.

Now I will list the trade that started up in Post Surrender Japan.

1 the "Baby Pearl" camera for GI's was produced by using military disused lenses.

2. "The Rabbit" this was a scooter was developed made from former fighter planes for Nakajima aircraft now re-named Fuji Industry.

3. Chewing gum factories were "set up" and there were as many as 400 companies!

5. "Greetings from Tokyo" Christmas cards were produced and reproductions of woodblock prints were made in their scores for the American military to send home during the winter season.

6. Cigarettes and tobacco industries started up. This served the GI's with no shortage of Japanese brands to chose from as well as their own makes.

7. Alcoholic beverages   were offered which the Government monopolized owning a share in the tobacco sales as well. "Old Brandy" was also included in the merchandising of drinks.

8, Rice rations dis-appeared and from 1946 the "era of the flour" started up away from rice eating. A "Home Baker" from an electrical company in Osaka was an early pioneer in bread baking.

9. There was a dress making boom copying the latest western style garments which was the obvious status symbol away from the drab anti western dress of the pre-war years. Dress making schools, fashion schools and style books suddenly bloomed in spite of the difficult times. The broad shouldered American look became the fashion and was most copied, being the rage of the day.

Springing from a lighter and happier frame of mind, all things bright "alongside exhaustion" being a code word for those times emanated in these early years after the War." Publishing houses recovered quickly above all other commercial sectors and paper kept running out as it was in short supply up to 1951. It is worthwhile noting that by the war's end, 300 publishing houses existed. Within eight months, there were almost 2000!

Writing was placed into publication which ran along these lines:

"The war which we had believed to be just was lost, our writings about victory turned into the wastepaper basket, and we young editors plunged into depths of despair..." The same must be true of your readers. Since you believed in war and dedicated yourselves to the home front, forgetting the seasons and youth and dreams, your shock must have been all the greater. This editorial leaving the press said that "tomorrow's Japan did not permit wallowing in confusion and perplexitiy." It goes on committing youth to bear to the duties of building a "new Japanese culture" to establish a nation of culture and peace.

Even the most difficult "road of thorns" there is a ray of light. Modern civilization must be met and better understood was the answer to the allegation of Japanese malaise. Jummin "The People" "magazine denounced the former regime of militarists, landlords, zaibatsu and emperor – centred bureaucratic system." They upheld a belief in democracy as seen and believed by the people's rights movement during another period in time. Their belief in the Meiji Reformation was in line with the ideal that one day there would be a peaceful Japan. Although Russian literature was read and Marxism became a favorite political stand amongst many writers, "we can understand better the perception of the Marxist school and their ideologies which must help Japan identify itself with a basic society for social justice and prevention or end of tyranny". It is to remember that Marxism is Communism, and before the war, they were not accepted. They were most often put into prison for writing their beliefs for sale. One such writer was Ozaki whose arrest in October 1941 proved he was a spy working for the Kremlin and who between the time of his arrest in October 1941 up until his execution in November 1944 at the age of 43, had passed on information to Richard Sorge, whose reports had provided the Soviet Union with invaluable information about Japanese strategic thinking before the attack on Pearl Harbor. He was the only Japanese to be formally tried for treason during the war, an extraordinary traitor in the eyes of the Japanese prior to August 15th 1945-a remarkable hero and martyr figure thereafter!

His famous letters were attractive and even the "hanging Judge" who decided on his death, believed him, nonetheless, as a true patriot and a man of virtue and ideals. Ozaki became for many a man who epitomized "peaceful universalism" and "utopia", that the Japan the Japanese tried so hard to find through the decades was the "bright new world" which was romantic and loving at the same time. His writings and thoughts were considered revolutionary at the time. He is the writer of "Love is like a shower of stars" which remained a bestseller for a long time. Even his wife Eiko, herself wrote a title of an essay called "I believe that dawn is approaching," containing hopes and dreams of a world more at peace with itself than the time she wrote it. Ozaki is known for his humanism and care of people, which was not well taken by the Communists. He wrote about love and romance in the wake of defeat. He was a sophisticated man and an unfaithful husband, finding it a bourgeois existence with his wife and only daughter. He cared little in reality for the "family state" and led quite a clandestine life and eventually ended his life in prison. However, at the end he wrote many letters to his wife and daughter from prison and shared his thoughts with them. He was affectionate to them both which is not at all a typical Japanese characteristic.

A scientist names Nogai Takashi, was victim of radiation sickness in Nagasaki, where he lived as a Christian. His two children gave forth the rending of a famous book called NAGASAKI NOKANE (The Bells of Nagasaki). Not only a scientist he was also a medical doctor. His wife had died during the bombing of Nagasaki. People like Helen Keller visited his sick bed as well as Emperor Hirohito of Japan. In 1950, his book, the Bells of Nakagasaki was made into a movie which was most popular. Nogai understood the bombings of Hiroshima and Nagasaki to be imposed intervention from the Divine. He said this about it: "Was not Nagasaki the chosen victim, the lamb without blemish, slain as a whole-burnt offering in an altar sacrifice, atoning for the sins of all nations during World War 11?"By nature, Nogai was a pacifist and it is true to say, the Japanese found him fatalistic and slightly unpalatable, his writings emerged just at the time the war crimes tribunals were held. He was considered as father (scientist), doctor-a victim of the nuclear bombed city of Nagasaki dying like a martyr and therefore saintly in their eyes.

Norman Mailer who wrote "The Naked and the Dead" could not contemplate a sale release as opportunity would have otherwise returned financial to him. This was due to the release of many letters and poems written from the World War Japanese pilots. Writers kept serious note of their remembrances without losing their orientation, realizing their goal was to seek out the peace for now and for a future. This would regain the stable and real world of a Japan emerging out of the troubles in a world gone mad during the war days. It is true it took Japan time after the terrible and humiliating defeat already suffered.

Indeed it must be true to say that the sharp contrast from war ideologues to the bright and democratic future was the future held as the "transitory bridge between the eras."

Clarity of purpose, purity of motive had been the cause célèbre and reason during the war years. Japan was from then on, to be the "Light of Asia" used as a propaganda slogan which worked well over the war years. Other slogans of that time were such wording as "Extinguish America and Britain and make a Bright World Map" or such wording of propaganda machines as a" fighting bright and strong" nation in war. Their legitimacy and their fight to the end was never questioned or used in an improper connotation and their belief that the war was fought to serve the country. Similarly, after the war, there was never any confusion that their new objective was to regain stability and useful means to serve the country which was ruined and destroyed, for the future of a brighter and better tomorrow. They promised the occupying forces just as genuinely to adhere to the new anti-military code of their days in war, and make drastic changes to rebuild a nation for peace, as well as a nation for culture

Young Prince Akihito practiced in this exercise was to be Japan's process to build "a New Culture tied to a radiant past." As he explains, "it was like emptying out an old valise and filling it with new things." It was going to be a "new age" from culture, democracy to new youth and new self-government with new freedom. "The new culture tied with the radiant past was the new order transferring a greater and brighter Japan for a renovation that had been in the plan since the 19th century. The transition was appropriated at this time to be the objective of that next generation.

Had history of the Meiji Reformation changed with the hierarchy exchanging from the old feudal samurai system to the Government of the Imperial State, so would the changes existing side by side with the American practice to legalize by central democratic government, see how Japan was an old master at knowing and accepting very big changes as history had already done in the 19th century and even before that. The continuity of the change was on a par with the understanding of the state of rule by the occupation of their forces. However, it was never the objective of the occupation to colonize the country of Japan.

One remembers another time when the "gunboat diplomacy" of an unequal and unfair treaty was forced through by the western powers in which Japan mildly agreed to accept the challenge of isolating the old feudal system. It is said that "conspiracy theories" became a symbol of continuity between the "epochs of war and peace…"Japan accused often enough the imperialist states from the west or the "caring communists" on the other hand. However history now dictates that the real conspirators were the military cliques who took over and were behind the greatest conspiracy putting Japan into full war and World War. In the days of the war, few would have described the war at the time as comparable to waste. However in hindsight the reality of the present day war on the front is the war of waste which some believe is often glorifying a new and unholy god! The order of one generation is taken over by the order of the new generation. The "old order" never really died. The new way is powerful and dangerous enough to foresee the crime waves of pedestrians in the streets as gangland warfare started up it's course of destruction worse than anything from West Side Story, which would be of a fairy tale quality in present times. Now they want welfare and more money than the blind could imagine possible. The war of want as the war of crime is almost unintelligible yet fierce and powerful that kills in waves by hundreds even thousands. Serbians flushing out the ethnics for a greater Serbia (not forgetting this time around), the case of Rwanda or the minefields of Angola. This is a show of western want in the past present history for atrocity and its wars. The inconceivable wars of the cities is destroying that godly democracy earned through the ages now destabilized by a method of inhumanity and it's acts of rule, the greatest war of all enacted against the most innocent. One does not lament the past of pagan Rome, for it appears on the front pages and on the streets as the pavement once lined with gold is now too often spattered with innocent blood! It is the time for much crying and sorrow, but nothing survives an era gone by, for the "new order" was put out of action and destroyed. This was the astonishing crime in Srebrenica by Serbs who killed the young Muslims. Criminals walk more freely now than they would have historically recorded and even Nostradamus would be defeated today by the "signs of the times" and the freedom seekers pitched volleys to secure it. "Let's go crazy" is not a joke. Hitler would appear to have been a martyr in a new order of   white supremacist and their racist rules leading the way to get rich fast by bully methods and brutality unspoken of or little mentioned in a police like state. Their rights and their taking of the law into their own hands force belief that they are all above the law! How unfortunate the nations have become if this is the general system to match one's aggressive feelings of the day! This is a price to have the reward much sought for, being the price for freedom. Scenes of immoral behavior standing behind one fence might prove the economic fall has given way to the blackmails and conspiracies watching democracy's death. Women's belief of a pagan good, has made them idle and complacent to the understated course of lazy opportunism and exploitation. Like a pre-war state, they offer their bodies as a recourse to gain illegally, benefits of earnings which is given a "blind eye" in an eventual count down to a futuristic "bomb shell" to engage in those frustrations. It could be that certain men or women can no longer accept a more conformed unification with the order of life and government as before. The mental health act are capable enough to enlist this on a program for hate, for the sake of not coping effectively with the traders of "illegal earnings" a power house unto itself. It has gone a far way since the times of World War 11 yet looking at my reading there is no doubt the similarity of those post war days have effectively been reviewed and re-enacted as unlikely as it sounds.

CHAPTER 4
THE LEGENDARY JAPAN

Let me now talk of the legend of Japan and it's historic religion. Shinto believes in the sun goddess "Amaterasu". The way of the subject was "Shimmu no Michi" a national policy - to be loyal to the Emperor in dismissal of self, thereby supporting His Throne and Imperial State combining the Heavens with the Earth and lastly denied all renunciation against his sacredness as Emperor Hirohito of Japan, whose war was holy." The Occupation settled the uncertain future of the Imperial Family and it's Household, by simply reinstating the Emperor and his Household as the head and culture of the new democracy. Under the new Constitution as written by the Americans, they kept the Emperor as "symbol of the state and of the unity of the people..."Hereditary privilege was confirmed by the "symbol, as the sovereign and head of that patriarchal authority. Only males could accede to the Throne. This led the Emperor to hold in his power the right of incarnation of racial purity and "cultural homogeneity."The separation of Church and State, claimed that the High Priest of the "indigenous Shinto religion" would practice their rights of "divine ancestors worship" at the great Ise Shrine. He was to fulfill all that was meant to be the image of "timeless" essence that set Japan apart from other peoples and their culture by their superiority. The Showa era began with Hirohito's ascending the Throne in 1926 and ended in the Showa era in 1989 when he died at the age of 89. "Communists stumbled and made fools of themselves when it came to the Emperor" it has been noted.

When Ambassador grew tried at the time of post surrender Japan, to denounce the Emperor calling for his end." Hirohito will have to go", was his commitment. He was under the calls from the Allied Nations who wanted to accuse him of being a war criminal and indite him for signing the Declaration of War. Yoshida Shigeru saw how MacArthur as "great benefactor" not necessarily relying on his position to democratize Japan, but rather how he helped position and preserve the "Imperial Throne of the August Occupant in a time of unprecedented peril". The Supreme Commander's policies as far as the Emperor was concerned never moved and established his retention of the throne even before surrender.

Psychological war was played by the Allies on the Japanese. The American Fellers was an expert on Japanese psychology and knew eventually the attacks by Kamikaze would probably be activated understanding their belief in the "holy war". Where the Emperor was concerned, he realized how gangster militarists had taken over the decision of the high military next to the Emperor. In order to regain the peace and stability of the former Japanese Government before the War, and to entitle the high nobility who had reigned Supreme in these days, the "retention" of the Imperial Throne with Hirohito on it was the obvious move to make - that, nobody could deny.

Prior to surrender and before intelligence and reports were given by MacArthur 's men, an adoption of Lefcadio Hearn's "Japan-An Attempt at Interpretation" makes the one observation made into reports passed from one intelligence officer to another. They understood by a simple process of learning, that the essence of the unchanging timeless structure of Hirohito's command was always to be the sacred person with affinity to the Divine heaven. Americans took care never to use words to attack Emperor Hirohito or speak of him as an enemy, for this would only serve hostility yet again and would be considered an attack on His Imperial Majesty. They realized many would fight to the death in order to defend the Honor of Hirohito. The Occupation was only there to pave a more important role for the establishment of the new order of Government agreeable and compliant to the ways and wishes of the Imperial Throne and to Emperor Hirohito himself. During the time of the War, it was established as a fait accomplit, that the leadership of the military lay with gangster militants who had literally "betrayed their sacred leader." This was the way of thinking well after the defeat of Japan after the War. It was obviously this was the preferred understanding amongst the Americans. Fellers however felt inclined to think that Emperor Hirohito was not completely innocent of guilt, but realized that he had some sympathy for the causes escalating up to war. At the time when he was the only person and Head who could be indispensable to the closing of the Pacific War, which he must have known must finish and settle for a surrender for the sake of peace and a way forward out of a terrible crisis. They knew his potential as the worship divine who may have instigated the Pacific War. Being the Spiritual Head of his country, he was essential to their cause. This conclusion was wiser than declared at the time for it never changed the authority of the Allied Supreme Commander nor of the Emperor Hirohito of Japan. Japan could keep their country for themselves and their Head of State unmoved by the changes undertaken to bring back the centralization of a democratic state.

The Showa era died with the death of Emperor Hirohito in 1989. Crown Prince Akihito succeeded him chosing the reign title of Heisen from the Chinese classics Shi JI (Book of History and Shi Jing era,(Book of Documents) a time for hope for achieving "peace" everywhere in "heaven and on earth, at home and abroad." During his reign, Japan's booming economy came to a grinding halt and recession took over. His time was an unsettled and less prosperous one and the irrelevance of the MIDDLE classes, which had been a greater part in the rebuilding and restabilizing of postwar Japan, was now held in question. They challenged the national homogeneity and validity of it, and showed a lack of contentment almost to the point of bitterness. It has been recorded that at the same time, the Soviet Union was going through international collapse. Japan at the time of postsurrender was coming out of a critical time and engaged itself with a future prospect to create a "new Japan" for reconstruction. This was the new identity and the new plan.

CHAPTER 5

MACARTHUR

General MacArthur took on his role as a substitute feudal lord and issued edicts with imperious panache, and brooked no criticism. He was supreme commander but never saw Japan over which he presided. He was obliged to charter Japan back on course and open it up again as a role model of friendliness and sympathy after the devastation they had suffered by the bombings of Hiroshima and the Christian community of Nagasaki, both blown by an A-bomb. He had to impose certain rules so that eventually Japan would be back on their feet again and in working order. He rarely socialized or met Japanese people. I do not know if this was a precaution to secure and safeguard his person as a ruling American Supreme Commander. When his day ended, he went back home always traveling between his home and HQ and home again. He watched newsreels and footages of recent news in Japan. Apart from this, he watched old movies usually American westerns.

Occupation people realized afterwards that this period in time proved something else about them. Many viewed them extremely conceited and arrogant, using their power and authority every inch of the way making themselves neither helpful nor popular. However all this was to eventually change.

In every war one experiences dehumanization. The Japanese were studied in clinical analysis under a theme called "know your enemy" by the War department before the surrender." They had stereotyped the Japanese as brutal, sadistic fanatical "monkey-men" and the Americans as mob-lynching, gangsters practicing race riots."

The feudal Imperial family were left alone and remained in their state of honor without the military support as displayed by the War. How different from the present notions of the theory that annihilism when practiced against a given monarchy in an overthrow is nothing other than a show of mob lynching, gangsterism and inhuman racist supremacy which reminds us how we learned to correct this through time and through better understanding and international cooperation. If history did not get corrected in the advancement of better education than this, it is not proved that it was the fault of Japanese people. The Japanese have proved to be "reliable, industrious, thrifty, brave, aggressive and honest." The honest truth is they are no different from other people from other countries.

The Meiji Reformation had set up a Government which the Occupation Forces of General MacArthur could change giving Japan a Japanese Government instead of the East-West "hybrid" born from the midwives "Satsuma-Cho". The hermaphroditic government had to be over-ruled and changed for a Government for Japan and its' pure race.

We have established that many were born from prostitution during the Post Surrender era of Japan and many children were illegitimate. This is not an unusual event or a course much less an accident…During the Post Defeated epoch, there were many prostitutes and it can be said that it was natural that many were born from them. They never had quite the same rights as a child born legitimately, however they could be considered rightful individuals with a right to live.

This is the age of the great drug war which is like the old war fought in the former Indochina between the Vietnamese and the French all over again as happened in the 19th century. There was once a French film declared brilliant with Catherine Deneuve called "Indochine" which must reveal and reward many, to understanding the war and the troubles of that conflict which was essentially a terrible Drug War. If they bothered to see this impressive movie which came out in the early 1990's, they would have foreseen an ultimatum there in that film related to the eventual falls and blackmail of any Drug War. Formerly, President Bush Senior drew it on a map while he still retained his Presidency in the United States after the first Gulf War, that this would be the greater part of the future wars of most nations, including crime wars. He bothered to mention that much of the problem might stem from bullies taking over most of the war crimes and troubles of any country involved in the greatest threat to humanity being the drug war. I have drawn on this as part of the history of post Gulf War era of 1990, for records will show the importance of the long list of wars to be overcome before the return of government can be restored.

CHAPTER 6

JAPANESE WAR CRIMINALS

There were two classes of war criminals. There was Class A and then Class B. All of them were not necessarily Japanese. There were Taiwanese indicted persons as many as 173, as well as 148 Koreans of whom over 40 were executed. The allegations of their crimes were such cruel and gruesome crimes that they were the first to go. Chinese Communists subjected around 1000 Japanese prisoners to intensive "re-education" during and after the war. Some were never brought to trail until 11 years after defeat. There were lessons learned. The Tokyo Tribunal it was noted by those standing accused of war crimes that they were the lower ranks of soldiers who realizing they were to be blamed and knowing this would be used for execution in lieu of the higher military and authority of the war years. Only a small number of high army and navy officers, a few bureaucrats, or captains of the war economy, civilians whose attachment to ideologues worsened as crimes against humanity occurred, with the consent of politicians of the time. There were as well academics, even medical personnel who sought to pump up racial arrogance and military fanaticism. It was a case where the average soldier on the front line stood to face a death sentence for the sake of saving the high military and their authorities. We can say that Japan's Nuremberg started on 3rd May 1946. The German Nuremberg Trails started on 20th November 1946. The Tokyo Tribunal continued for 31 months. A caption read "We hanged them because they used war as an instrument in national policies and politics."

Class A dealt with crimes against peace, which was the planning and preparing of war in which part of the criminal activity involved the violation of international law, treaties, or betrayal of agreements, assurances and participating in a common conspiracy for the accomplishment of any of the foregoing.

Conventional war crimes were such violations of the laws or customs of war:

Crimes against humanity were reenactments of murder, extermination, enslavement, deportation and other inhumane acts committed during or before the war. The laws enforcing violation of domestic law planning a "conspiracy to forge acts of crime against those they rule, in an effort to execute that plan to betray the peace of the nation at large." In the meanwhile, the Nuremberg Trails were convened by the allies who must punish the Nazis for the genocidal policies that came to be the Holocaust. In Tokyo, the indictment-crimes against humanity was treated with "conventional war crimes" or just plain "murder."

Similiarly the Allied Trail of Nazi, Germany, the Tokyo Tribunal was said in a few words to conjure up the meaning of the trails, deliberation and sentence by BVA Roling, a Dutch judge at the Tokyo Trail who said "international law was en route to banning war and rending it a criminal offense."

Although the notoriety of these trails have been heard of since the days of the end of World War 11 in both Europe and in the Pacific, we realize too sadly, that war is a crime. In a way, nobody can be blamed for warring on the warred, and be told anything other than they have committed crimes against humanity but did it for their country which is not necessarily a crime. It is a "blame situation but a blameless one." It contradicts as well as confirm that war is about crime. The leaders are the devil in disguise, giving with one hand and taking away with the other, and making you pay at the end of a lost war, for the criminal they engage in sentencing you to.

Class B war criminals

Of this class of war criminals, 984 were condemned to death. There were 475 life sentences, and 2944 limited prison terms. 1018 were accounted for and found. 279 were never brought to trail. Most of them were enlisted men from the lower levels of the "chain of command."

At the same time there was a lot written by educators and journalists about the West who taught that we must learn from each other, and pray for each other's welfare and do with each other according to the "laws of nature and man." This was looked at with certain suspicion and after studying the said policy, realized that the law of nature said that the stronger nation could devour the weaker one, just as likely as the law of the jungle may be associated with threats or impositions by greater nations against a weaker one. Indeed it was "Jakuniku Kyoshoku" or the law of the jungle that mattered.

His question was "how could Japan avoid being crushed by the Western juggernaut?" His understanding further explained that military defense was absolutely essential to their cause: "when others use violence we must be violent too. "Japan must ask other Far Eastern countries to "reform themselves" so that they could defend themselves against any foreign attack to protect its borderlines. If they should refuse, he reasoned, Japan must "compel" them to. "Japan should be prepared to act ruthlessly." Japan, he felt, could not be a participating and waiting servant for the rest of it's neighboring countries. It must "break out of formation and join the civilized countries of the west on the path to progress. "We should not give any special treatment to China and Korea but should treat them in the same way as do the western nations" he said.

On the understanding that Japan was a player amongst the supremist western nations in the Far East, it was little wonder their success brought them to Korea where they exchanged hands in government and became the head leaders of this state. I will now explain how this came about. This was not to remain long in one time, however, it remains a fact that Tokyo had much invested in their new ideal world found in Korea, in exchange for Japanese protection under its sovereignty. It is also true that some Japanese found their "utopia" in their newly acquired state of Manchuria later on. They must fight hard to keep this their own "Manchukuo" and in spite of the demands of the Manchurian monarchy and the futility of their rights to oust the Japanese out of the newly discovered resort, the League of Nations decided eventually in favor of Japanese sovereignty in this state which returned greater rewards than any that could be discovered in their own country. They survived there, lived happily and became a state as wonderful as any "utopia" could be for the Japanese settlers! This was counter-balanced by the extraordinary war waged against China over an incident in Shanghai later on. All the past of that time will now be opened for the reader to understand, to see how the program would evolve into a war that should probably have been better avoided. However, risks were taken in no small measure. During the 19th Century, there was greater scope for wars to start and for them to stop without too much ado, with losses both sides. Everything was settled and agreed peacefully with strange documents called "Treaties". It was a different time, and the difference was that "things were done differently then!".

CHAPTER 7

KOREA

In 1894-1895, a war occurred in Korea. Kim Ok-Kyun "a young self-styled progressive leader" admired Japan's stand regarding western imperialism. He wanted to portray a similar government in Korea following the Meiji teachings. He wanted new ideas for a reformation that "would strengthen Korea and thus e#nable the kingdom to resist domination by outside powers that might also be hostile to Japan." He met Fukuzawa before the latters publication of "DATSU-ARON. Encouraged and supported, he led an organized coup against the Korean monarchy. He used weapons he had acquired in Japan. He and his followers stormed the royal palace 4th December 1884. The rebels seized King Kojong and killed many in his surrounding declaring an "independent and new pro-Japanese government." Korean conservatives held their ground and appealed to the Chinese army to strengthen and back up their fight. After three days of fighting they restored order back into the capital. "Kapsin Coup" had fallen. Kim left for Japan immediately, while angry Korean mobs seeking revenge killed 40 Japanese and burned their "legation down to the ground". Furthermore, they went up to Ito Hirobumi to calm things down. He was about to advance a new constitutional program and when delivered the news of the conflict with Korea, Ito immediately went to visit his counterpart in China. There he was told how the Great Powers considered Japan to be on "the wrong side of the moral fence." China too had problems with France in the Vietnamese fight to claim sovereignty over that state and with Great Britain moving closer to Burma, things were getting "hot." In April, 1885, Ito and Li reached an Agreement. The Tianjin Convention agreed that neither side would station troops in or go near the peninsular of Korea unless a written notice was made. Two arrests were made on Oi Kentaro and Fukuda Hideko for conspiracy to instigate a conflict and coup against the Korean Government. It forced Kim to flee to Shanghai as an exile.

In spite of his escape, agents of the Korean government murdered him in Shanghai. They took his body to Seoul where they dismembered his dead body as a warning to other would be reformers of the government. This was done regardless of protests from the Press and agents and members of the Japanese government. There was a peasants' march in which they demanded greater funding for the poor in Korea. There were religious cult members of a new religion springing up in Korea called Tonghkat. At this point King Kojong called for armed assistance from China. This was watched by the Japanese who quickly decided to take action as a top priority. The reason for their imperious reaction was simply a case whereby China had contravened the Tianjin Convention by their breaching it's signed Agreement with Tokyo, not long before, which resulted in British and Russian intervention regarding the Korean peninsula. In a Treaty, Tokyo offered Seoul protection rather than intervention in Korea's domestic and foreign affairs in order to put forward an increased possibility to achieve a strengthening of Korea under a Japanese influence to better the "rights of our merchants"… They promised greater protection and extended their influence over Korea. They wanted as a strong contact for Japan, while at the same time, increase trade for Japanese merchants. This done, they returned to Korea where they met unfair hostility from the Chinese and skirmishes with their forces broke out provoking Tokyo into officially declaring War on China on 1st August 1894!

Since 1890, Yamagata had built up arms storages which prepared Japan for a war. The Japanese forces advanced against the overwhelming Chinese at Pyongyang on 16th September, and won a decisive naval battle. The next day another battle ensued whereby they confronted the Chinese navy at Yalu River, seized Port Arthur on 12th November and on 12th February 1895, destroyed the Chinese fleet at Wei Haiwei, where the unfortunate Chinese Admirals killed themselves after their humiliating defeat.

With greater impact, Yamagata realized his opportunity to extend the campaign into China proper, despite the worrying costs of the war and it's efforts leaving the possibility of retaliation by the western countries living in the mainland of China.

Ito wanted to stop all hostilities and sit at a table to negotiate and settle their differences with Li.

In 1895, Li this time around, ten years after signing the first Tianjin Agreement, had to journey to meet Ito in Japan. Their conversation and the conduct leading up to signing the second Agreement must be in the English language. Ito was bi-lingual and had the advantage of being fluent in English. English must be considered the official language signed by both sides at Shimonoseki. At the conference demands were slapped on as demands to the Chinese Li by Ito were struck out as hard negotiations commenced. They were as follows:

1) Full and complete independence and autonomy of Korea;

2) Cession of Manchuria province of Liaoning as well as Taiwan;

3) Territory of Pescadores islands;

4) Payment of 500million yen as indemnity;

5) Opening for trade for Yangzi River and trade with four trading ports;

Although Li suffered and spoke carefully about their demands for an Agreement, a Japanese fanatic shot Li and wounded him below the eye.

As a result, the Japanese demands were forced into another condition meaning their demands had to be watered down. Ito agreed to lose most of the indemnity and accept one third, and asked afterwards for a territorial claim of Manchurian peninsula of Liaodong. The rest of his demands were accepted and the Treaty of Shimonoseki was signed 17th April 1895. This made Japan the first non-western power as a main player and therefore an imperial power.

Japan became the central Asian figure in revising treaties amongst the western powers.

Great Britain held stubborn prejudice against treaty rights until they saw an opportunity to spike a Russian ambition regarding North Asia.

The Anglo-Japanese Commercial Treaty of 1894 was signed in London on 16th July 1894. This meant they agreed to leave their settlements in Japanese cities and would do away with "extraterritoriality" within a span of five years.

By 1897, the other treaty powers, impressed with Japan's new military prowess, also agreed and entered negotiations by recognizing Japan's tariff and autonomy which completed it's course of equalization of all relations by 1911.

The casting aside of "unequal treaties" gave rise to newer and stronger patriotic feelings in Japan. Not only was the signing of the Shimonoseki Treaty a great success which amassed a greater fortune for Japan but, Japan had become a main player on the world stage regarded by the then Empire Builders of that generation of men in the late nineteenth century. This was considered a remarkable achievement. Tokutomi Soho stated in a few words the great victory Japan had won over China saying "The West now realizing that civilization is not a monopoly of the white man" – that the Japanese too " had a character suitable for great achievements the world." However, the treaty of Shimonoseki was short lived due to the intervention by St Petersburg advising Tokyo to give up Liaodong peninsula and return it back to the Chinese. This was backed by France and Germany who agreed to this "friendly counsel". As a result, Japan looked to British and American intervention only to be advised of the futility and uselessness of disagreeing with their "friendly counsel." On 5th May, Japan agreed to returning Liaodong back to China! There was no choice about it. The Triple Intervention soon cancelled the Treaty of Shimonoseki which had been the pride of achievement of Tokyo. After the 5th May, Russia continued their stance and demands for a way forward under their protectorate. Russia was soon meddling in Korea's domestic affairs. The Japanese diplomatic corps got nervous when they witnessed Korea's Queen Min who "emerged as a rallying point for anti-Japanese sentiment." This had averse effects on the Japanese side which provoked a terror attack on the Queen in the morning of 8th October, when the Japanese crew accompanied by Korean trainees broke into the Palace and stabbed her to death, dragging her body into the garden, where they doused her corpse with kerosene and lit a match! This in turn provoked further anti -Japanese sentiment by their Kong Kojong, who fearing for his life, by now, requested the attendance of the Russians to secure his position in the capital. By putting Russian guards to protect him and Seoul, the Korean Government handed them a grant and allowed them mining rights and timber rights in the northern peninsula so sought out and fought for.

The outrage of the murder didn't help the Japanese Government who at first denied the murder! However the eye witness reports by the Americans proved that their truthfulness and explanation justified the wrong-doing of the Japanese attack that night on the poor Queen of Korea. Japan soon realized the harshness of their international credibility which had been shot down and their reliable reputation hit them by force,with the result that the Russians seeing their opportunity exploited it against the better reserve of the Koreans troops . They held a case against Japan. This ultimately resulted in the worst situation of all. The Russians literally helped themselves to Manchuria anyway, which had been ceded to Japan at the time of the signing of the Treaty. The Russians kept up their "hard deal" maintaining all right to the rail operations from Lake Baikal westward across Manchuria to Vladivostok on the eastern Railway which was about to open. After two years, the Russians verily bullied the Chinese into giving them a 25 year leasehold on Liaodong Peninsula and permission to build, linking the naval base at Port Arthur to the new Chinese Eastern Railway at Harbin. This led the Russians to occupy Manchuria, forcing both Korean and Chinese Governments to accept this as the settlement.

Japan stood united "in the shame of Liaodong" and the growing presence of Russia in Northern Asia (Korea). Tokyo's interest in obtaining a better response to protecting Korea from Western Powers was a "determined effort which won them further military strength and presence" for the sake of preserving independence to the Liaodong Peninsula as well keeping a firmer grip on their own foreign policies. This was more costly but necessary. The Diet conceded to the request for better funding and paid out 24 million yen before the Sino-Japanese War, the cost estimated at 73 million yen in 1896 and 110 million yen the next year. The Japanese army had doubled in size and their fleet was the biggest in the whole of Asia.

Japan must win back respect by the other powers and earn a better diplomatic offensive. China was not prepared for any more conflicts as Peking and the rest of China was in the middle of the Boxer Rebellion. Japan's presence in an international gathering as a full member of the Beijing-Tianjin region , proved a success as part of the protection on cite to be amongst the nations protecting it's diplomatic personnel . The agreement was signed on 7th September 1901. By this Japan was given the right to station troops in Beijing-Tianjin region. In 1902, Japan reached another Agreement with Great Britain. In the Anglo-Japanese Alliance of 1902, the two nations agreed their privileges in China, and that Japan's special interests in Korea should provide enough back-up to support their concern in the event Russia took on an aggressive stance with military weight on either country.

The talks were negotiated according to the following:

1) Concerns of some 50,000 troops Russia had sent into Manchuria to protect Russian workers and their families during the Boxer Rebellion

2) If Russia could respect Japan's claims and interests in protecting Korea;

3) If Russia could observe Japan's claims to the independence and preservation of Korea.

The czar's delegates showed practically no enthusiasm for agreeing with any or part of these details and unfortunately this resulted in dismissing all potential settlement for a better co-existence due to their lack of observance and cooperation.

Although President Tokutomi felt shock and humiliation over the Triple Intervention, Japan's status had not been over-ruled due to the 1902 Treaty with Great Britain over the Russians. They were still considered major players of the nations.

Eventually in June 1903, seven professors from Tokyo University wrote to the President. Their statement was quoted in the newspapers which did urge "immediate war" to find a "fundamental" resolution to the Manchurian crisis, which might secure Japan's position in Korea.

They addressed the Emperor in a conference meeting on 4th February 1904. They agreed;

1) Japan's vulnerability under the siege by Russia of Manchurian territory gives Japan a chance to enhance it's political position amongst the Great Powers if they declared war on Russia.

2) On 6th February 1904, Japan severs diplomatic relations with Russia.

3) The Japanese navy attack Russian ships at Port Arthur.

4) 10th February of that year, the Emperor officially declares War on Russia during a visit to the Yasuniku Shrine.

General Nogi Maresuke, a hero of the Sino-Japanese War, leads his forces –the Third Army on to the Korean Peninsula in February and by March is occupying Dairen, so that by August 1904, Port Arthur is under siege. By New Year, it falls and delivered to the Japanese.

The long and terrible battles lasted long and furiously and the carnage was a foreshadow of things to come as seen in World War 1. The army had lost too many officers and men and as well had depleted most of it's arsenal to a more powerful and tougher Russian army. Admiral Togo Heichiro won a great victory in Spring 1905 that brought Russia to the negotiating table. Britain had blocked the Suez Canal from the Russian Baltic Fleet which had sailed from the Gulf of Finland with a determination to blast the Japanese out of Port Arthur. Due to the magnitude and seriousness of the blockade in Suez, this detour made their journey arduous and longer than necessary. They had to journey around Africa and across the Indian Ocean. Neutral ports closed in on them throughout their journey. In the confrontation between the two sides, the Russians were over-powered completely and their fleet sank. The Russo-Japanese War was a stalemate. The Emperor's armies could not hope to push back the czar's forces out of Manchuria and the Japanese could not be moved from the cities and surrounding territories run down by General Nogi. The Japanese asked President Roosevelt to prepare for a peace settlement and a peace conference was put together at Portsmouth, New Hampshire on 5th September.

On that day, Japan and Russia signed the Treaty of Portsmouth. This signed agreement made Japan victorious. The second clause stipulated;

1) Russia recognizes Japan's priority and interests in Korea and not oppose any measure protected for it, by Japan.

2) Liaodong Peninsula - the leasehold held by Russia was to be given back to Japan (referred to as the Kwangtung Territory).

3) It gave the czar's railroad and money and mining rights in Manchuria as well as sovereignty over half of Sakhalin to the Japanese.

The Japanese were victorious. It secured for itself a favorable prominence in the world in spite of indemnity which could not be met until the end of the war. The net amount they had to meet was a staggering 1.7billion yen.

CHAPTER 8
COLONIZING KOREA

Some Koreans welcomed Japanese modernization and their projects but others saw with certain prejudice what they understood to be an illegitimate take-over of their government and their economy. By 1905, the Japanese Government established an office for the silent partner of the Japanese Resident General. It was up to the Japanese to maintain law and order and if at all possible, help Korea settle in their foreign policies as managed by the new Resident General of Japan. Ito, took on this post and at the same time kidnapped the Korean King Kojong. I will now explain the sad story of the events that would lead to the complete ousting of the Japanese presence in Korea. The Korean Army was completely disbanded on 1st August. Ito and his thousands then started the reformation of the Korean currency and tax, as well as modernizing it's telegraph and postal system. At the same time trade was beginning to be processed and the rail link between Seoul and Pusan was completed which proved significant in the military operation which proved to be one which must not have failure for the sake of the important statement justifying the link up. Although the Japanese had moved to Korea by the hundreds from the countryside and farming areas, there was undisputed opportunities to trade on a long term basis for the new settlers. However the Big Businesses did not invest in any of these opportunities and search for trade. This was partly due to the history of the wars that had gone on for sometime about the Liaodong Peninsula. They rightly feared political instability. They pulled out of the enterprise as a consequence and did not attempt to cancel this from their suspicions about the politics of their northern neighbor. Above all, they feared war breaking out again on the Liaodong Peninsula.

However, King Kojong was unhappy with the restoration of the Japanese colonialisation of his country and by June 1907, made a somewhat unsuccessful Appeal to the International Community dispatching special secret envoys to the Second Hague Conference on World Peace to plead for a declaration on behalf of and supporting Korea and its' independence. However, with a failure to persuade them of Korea's rights during the Occupation by Japan and its military forces, a violent outbreak occurred that same summer against them and using gorilla fighters calling themselves the "righteous army! Koreans fought long and hard, and severe struggles broke out bringing the numbers of 18,000 Koreans dead, and 7000 Japanese fallen in their war, by 1910. The events came to a momentum when a Korean patriot gunned down General ITO Hirobumi, when he stepped off the train in Hartin, Manchuria. Eventually, a Treaty of annexation was signed on 22 August 1910. The colony and covenant renamed Korea Chosen, was made a colony of Japan, and the military appointee was the Governor General of Korea.

One must remember that between 1894-1904, there were "growing threats from the larger predator over the smaller nations imposing such deliberate anti- pacifist moves that the governments of both socialists and pacifists were extremely concerned about the hostilities between Russia and Japan." Japan found further support from other nations and due to their ability obtained both Taiwan and Sakhalin, managing the empire they sought, but at the same time, protected itself on the national front by having more of Asia supporting them. This popular movement gave good results and the eventual annexation of Korea gave them security, equity and first class status among the nations giving birth to a "new dawn of the new century" which gave promise of all they could hope for. This was the age of the acquisition of Empire. This was the fundamental essence of things to come in view of a later war in the Pacific starting with the invasion of Pearl Harbor. We cannot dismiss this historical fact as Japanese history teaches us to understand better and more clearly that the cause celebre was to obtain the fortunes and greatness of Empire. We now know how they could not win this Great War. It was a myth and an ideology that would come about only after the post war years of post defeated Japan, and the economic miracle so fought for, would eventually take place in the years to come. How did Japan start a war when so little money was available to match the army, navy and air force against the greater and more powerful United States of America? Wars are often fought to better the economy in strife, and the conditions for that end makes men sometimes go crazy. This may be an explanation of how wars start in the first place. The War of the Pacific was an elongation of the Empire Builders and their wars for victory, glory, empire, and wealth

CHAPTER 9

UNDER THE SHOGUNATE

Commodore Perry and his black ships wanted to open Japan for trade. It led to an end of self-imposed isolation. Although trade was accepted and trade barriers cut down, the foreigners knew little about the Japanese and other Asian countries. However, the Japanese knew more about the American than the American knew about the Japanese.

The Tokugawa Bafuku (or autocratic rule which did last for two centuries) had an ideology based on neo-Confucianism, of the 12th Century. It was created by a Chinese philosopher named Chu His, whose important role was to teach that natural order was of the greatest importance and that in complete obedience of and to authority, as far as the translation went from Chinese into Japanese. It was a measure exercising that purist ideal. The Emperor believed this rule was to define the dogma and teaching of Chu His making sure their belief was strictly adhered to by their followers and their people. They were like clerics or priests who were empowered to interpret the rules of heaven and though the teachers and doctors of Chinese medicine were Confucius. It was later challenged as the teachings from the West came to be based and founded on better science or medicine, and did attack the status of Confucianism. It is true to say at the same time that though Christians tried to be taught and to spread, Christianity, it was never accepted in spite of the Spanish and Portuguese missionaries. Dutch medicine was considered better than Confucian medicine and Nagasaki opened their doors firstly with Commodore Perry, than later as certain improvement was allowed in, the Japanese could buy foreign books by kindness of Tokugawa Yoshimuere. This gave Japanese people greater ability and therefore greater understanding with a faith to better power. There was conflict, when it was discovered that in principle Dutch medicine and science were better, resulting in the unavoidable non acceptance of the legitimacy of Confucian philosophy in a Confucian state. However purists and purism according to the legitimacy of Chu His teachings have never completely fallen out in Japan as now, it has been searched out by many from the West.

The Shogun was a military strongman who ruled Japan. The Emperor was a namesake who was like a secular ruler or Pope who might bless you. Fights were fought against the Shogun in the name of the Emperor. This was not illegal. Merging of church and state was to be a foundation of modern Japanese nationalism. They looked for the older ancient tradition and at the same time used the European and more modern model in the name of progress. It was the trade of trades and Japan opened its ports eventually for better acquisitions.

CHAPTER 10

MANCHURIA MANCHUKUO

The "real birthday of New Japan" began with the conquest of China at the turn of the century. "Bunmei kaika" - is a saying which inspired the colonial conquest as the ideal sign of ultimate greatness and modernity. No serious nation could be without an empire was the belief of Honda Toshiaki. After all a Sino-Japanese war had brought Japan closer to realizing the supremacy over Korea. As the empire was expanding and Japan served as modernizers of Asia, at the same time taking Taiwan and making it the "enlightened colonialism" it proved the greatness of Japan after they had defeated Imperial China at the same time dismissing those unequal treaties the West offered them in the past. Japan by now, was a nation to contend with, in military strength and newly found substance. "The lesson learned from Commodore Perry had born its dark fruit. "We can now summarize the three most important years when the reality poses the question as to how the Great War developed from 1931 with the Manchurian Incident, as well as 1937, with the China Incident, and finally 1941, with the attack on Pearl Harbor. The question is "when did the Japanese World War begin? "Was it in 1931, or 1937 or 1941? Daito Senso - were the words still used to explain the wars fought for the Japanese, for the liberation of Asia from Western Powers and their Empires. Others place greater importance on the Taiheiyo Senso as though there was no other war truly fought apart from the Great War against the United States with the attack on Pearl Harbor. However others refer to the colonial conquest beginning with Manchuria in 1931 which is often spoken of as the Fifteen year war.

Then the writer and intellectual former communist who turned into a right wing nationalist during the Taisho era, suggests by his theory that Japan entered the war as long ago as 1846 when the American James Biddle set afoot on Japanese soil only to be rebuked and roughed up by a guard, attempting to open relations and trade with Japan. He claims that since this time, Japan had paved its way into a war against the West and had stayed in war since this time. It is also to mention that security became a greater issue of defending this small nation against outside attacks which still remains a question mark now more than ever before and over most of the islands dotted here and there in the Pacific as well. If Tsunami could be the mischief maker to wreck havoc potentially anywhere in the world, than all nations must look for their own Kamikaze or Divine Wind or in fact God (in western terms) to save us all!

Hayashi chose to interpret the victimization of Japan as victims of Western powers whose wicked ways forced Japan to stand up to them for the Asian people. One of the chief promoters for the war against China insisted that Commodore Perry and his black ships were entirely to blame for the whole episode leading up to challenging as a rival might do taking on their aggression and wars which until this time had never existed in Japan. Japan had been pulled in, he claims into a "system of big power-rivalry."

The Manchurian incident had started up on September 18th 1931. Although a warlord governed Manchuria, as "a fiefdom" the Japanese found themselves in a position of advantage. The Japanese Kwantung army controlled this area which included the South Manchurian Railway of which the main cities of Harbin and Mukden were a part of this link. The port cities of Dalian and Port Arthur were already under direct Japanese governance. The army however wanted more territory! Things at home were not good as an economic downfall hit Japan hard, and anti-capitalist violence took hold of some of the younger officers and men. Coup d'etats by right wing "zealots" moved against businessmen and politicians in Tokyo. In the meanwhile, in China, the leader of the Party was Chang Kai -Shek. He tried to move north to try unifying the nation under one national government. The Chinese saw Manchuria as part of China, the Japanese in spite of the treaties before, did not. They saw Manchuria as a "lawless no man's land" and Japan wanted it to be theirs for putting in order. Manchuria had always been a part of China. However the Japanese claim brought the two in a war about the territorial claim of the Japanese as a sovereign ruler over that state. Manchuria had been part of China for almost three centuries and there was no doubt the Chinese had a legitimate claim to that territory. The fact was that though China had fallen into lawlessness, it did not permit the Japanese to take them over. However, a plot stirred up enough trouble against the Chinese by blaming them for blowing up a railway line near Mukda on 18th September 1931. The Japanese called the Chinese soldiers bandits. Because it was the duty to secure the Kwantung army of Manchuria, the Japanese attacked. Within six months, Manchuria was in the hands of the Japanese.

In the 1930's many Japanese officials, revolutionary "desperado" and "right wing dreamers" lived in Manchuria. A certain Lt Col. Ishiwara Kanji, like his forebear Kita Ikki, an intellectual mentor, wanted to transform the take-over of Manchuria into a "paradise" state! This was a dream which was about to materialize at a price. At home, the politicians and party heads realized they had no control over their army in Manchuria and could not calm down the fighting going on. Though their nerves were not good and tension grew concerning the battles for territorial claims, there was nothing they could do to stop them. Not even the Emperor could dispel their fears and the nations "courtiers and chiefs of staff" were told not to antagonize his armed forces, lest they rebel and create disturbances at home…The opposition party leader, Seiyukai, complained how the government showed little observation to security matters and were insufficient in regard to vigilance. The Japanese troops began to move into Manchuria from Korea and at this point, the Prime Minister of Japan, resigned. His part was taken over by Inukai Touyoshi, who tried withholding any recognition of Manchuria as an independent state, and this had serious consequences. The anti-Japanese sentiment by Chinese troops provoked an attack in Shanghai by Japanese marines on Chinese troops. Though the Chinese resistance was stronger than expected, the army of Japan was called in to help the marines. Inukai was unable to control the intervention of the military. He approached the Emperor appealing for his help. He attempted one more time to stop Japanese action from escalating violence in Shanghai. This proved fatal for him. He was gunned down by navy fanatics in his own home! The assassination in 1932 of Inukai altered the rights of a civilian cabinet due to the forceful debates of Ishiwara Kanji and some of the highest military officials of Tokyo, who had participated in the conspiracy against Manchuria and Shanghai, otherwise related and known as the "incidents".

On the other hand, in Europe, the Nazi take-over of Germany had produced the leadership of their Fuhrer. The Emperor of Japan could never change his role, and as long as he was there, he was the divine guidance with a system put in place by the Meiji Restoration which would remain intact. Until 1932, the Court was made up of Government posts, Diet, bureaucracy and the armed forces. Since the 1920's, this had been the established order, but now, it had come to an end and politics was to turn around courtiers, army and navy chiefs, bureaucrats "whose decisions were often forced on them by fanatical subordinates."

The Japanese occupied and settled in Manchukuo the new name given to Manchuria. Though the Chinese tried to keep this state from falling entirely, under a Japanese rule, they could not out-reason the Japanese points of view regarding the economic growth and potential trade they might have with mining and railway connections. There was the existence at the same time of the Manchurian emperor Pu Yi, "the hapless last scion of the Qing dynasty who "would be advised" by discreet, capable and benevolent Japanese officials. "In the meanwhile, the Japanese claimed that China was "not a viable state" and therefore gave Japanese every right to protect their interests in taking a firm hand in the north. "No matter how much the Japanese accorded respect to the Chinese emperor, Manchukuo was not even a puppet state, but a colony, pure and simple. Manchukuo officials were Chinese, but the appointments and policies were entirely in the hands of the Kwangtung army. This directly resulted in the take-over and the Chinese government who were extremely unhappy by this state of affairs, called in the League of Nations from an international court and asked for the investigation against the Japanese league on any claims and merits to deserve isolation of Manchuria from the rest of China. Britain had certain sympathy for Japan. Travel writers and visitors alike were impressed by the neatness, orderliness and cleanliness of the Japanese settlements in comparison to the general chaos and filth of the Chinese towns. Japanese soldiers could be arrogant and rough, but the railway hotels were "splendid" and were comparable to Mussolini's Italy, for a reason such as - "the trains always ran on time "The League of Nations was prepared to look into Chiang Kai Shek's request to return Manchuria back to mainland China. The delegation investigating this case was led by Lord Lytton who concluded the Japanese claim "was spurious". This rendered further outpourings of self-pitying propaganda "whereby the West was ganging up on Japan, together with China. At the end, at the League of Nations the Chief delegate being Matsuoka Yosuke, made an "astonishing speech" comparing Japan to Jesus Christ, martyred and crucified by public opinion."

Manchukuo was a way out and a place to restore a sense of a playground for many left-wing idealists who found work in the railway company thinking often of how to help reform and modernize Asia and its masses. There was attraction held in Manchukuo and Taiwan, for engineers and architects. The idealism held by the social scientists evolved around the gathering of the political party Kyowakai or the Concordis Society . These were the five races living together in harmony and following the rule of the Japanese. Included amongst the races involved in this cooperation were the Japanese, Manchus, Koreans, Chinese, Russians. The Japanese felt more comfortable living in Dalian or Mukden than ever in Osaka or Tokyo. Novelists, essayists as well as film-makers all gathered together in Manchukuo to write about or film. This Asia had such an idealism which appealed to the senses of many if not more from all walks of life. The newness and modernity of their newly found state as well as the speed of the trains and the finest parks found in Dalian, not to forget night life of Harbin were the perks and the undisputed great change offered far away from the former Marxist sentiments with anti-capitalist beliefs. Their belief no longer involved itself in National Socialism.

Tenko-"conversion" a communist writer Kobayashi Takiji, refused to renounce his political beliefs, and he died in prison in 1933. He was believed to have been tortured to death. This kind of barbarity was not common. Most communists were put into prison but were not tortured because they were prepared to renounce communism.

CHAPTER 11

THE CHINA INCIDENT
FEBRUARY 23, 1936

Imperial officers decided to call a strike in Tokyo. This was a direct attack against the Government and Imperialists found a way of comforting the hardships of the people who suffered a lot from negligence and welfare living in the northwest where a slump had hit the worst. The impoverishment levels were very severe, that young girls were being sold to pimps running the countryside to find a supply to take back to the brothels in the city. The army was offering farm boys a refuge. A brighter boy called Kita Ikki was fired with an enthusiasm and obsession for a pure and religious worship of his country a kind of imperialist national whose fundamentalism was to go a long way. Over 1000 men tried to take over central Tokyo. The finance minister was assassinated in his bedroom, as were the Lord Privy Seal and the Inspector General of military education, a control faction man. President Okada escaped with his life, his brother-in-law mistaken for him. Pamphlets were passed around in Tokyo undisputedly expressing a certain amount of emotional but sincere apologies but with reasons for their rebellion on behalf of the rebels who had caused such a terrible commotion.

Emperor Hirohito was not impressed. He said quite rightly, the attempted coup was a "direct attack on the establishment around him." ..."This kind of insubordination had to be stopped..." The navy was called in to restore order. The rebels tried to storm the palace to get the better part of their bad feelings known to both the Emperor and "his evil advisers." By 29th February, it was all over, and the rebels surrendered, the control faction having firmly taken back the control of the government.

Although Japan had nearly succumbed to a violent revolution it was saved just at the right time. A new government must be appointed and the new cabinet had to be approved by army and navy ministers. Hirohota Koki, a former diplomat was chosen as the new President. He must do the bidding of the army and navy ministers. He raised the military budget and signed an anti-communist alliance with Nazi Germany. Meanwhile, in China, the troops were getting restless again. The new President Hirohoto couldn't control them like his two predecessors before him. The Conservatives in the Diet were not ready to launch a war against China. Prince Konoe Fumimaro who had grown up with Hirohito and was a regular golf partner with good connections in the military together with his right wing intellectual friends was not himself a pro war man. He was an extreme anti-communist and held racial prejudices for his time. He was a man and a Prince who saw the world in terms of racial conflict between East and West. He looked to a Japan which held back domestic conflicts in a totalitarian Japanese state. Not even Prince Konoe could restrain his troops in China. The war with China was never actually declared. It began with the China incident." On 7th July 1937 when a Japanese private went to relieve himself on the Marco Polo Bridge near Peking, then continued walking in a demilitarized zone. He had been gone for a long time when his Commander proposed a search warrant for him. The Chinese official suggested a "joint search". The Japanese commander took this on as an insult. Violence broke out and spread quickly to other parts of China. It was Prince Konoe who "sought revenge and teach a lesson to the Chinese forcing them to reflect how a full scale war had started up which had never been the intended plan. He was out to stay neutral in his position yet get public opinion on his side. There was by the summer of 1937, a horrible battle near Shanghai in which Chiang Kai Shek met the forces from Japan. The city was bombed and 250,000 Chinese fell to their deaths, some of them civilians. They say in a description of the Battle of Shanghai that the rivers changed the "color of the sea" by the taking of such a lot of blood. "Blood flowed like a river."

By November, a balloon floated above Shanghai saying that one million Japanese had landed. More Japanese troops landed in the Bay of Hazhhou. The battles were about to recommence and the bloody march to Nanking was to be another starting point for this, in a strike against Chiang Kai Shek. The Nanking massacre in December 1937 was one of the most atrocious and brutal scenes of the Japanese war in China. Like zealots, the Japanese diplomats did what they could to ask Tokyo to pull out and stop the terror and the fighting. However nothing was done. Nobody knows exactly how many Chinese died in the massacres, but many believe it to be about 250,000. A terrible monster was forging ahead in wars against China, Manchukuo, the Philippines, Singapore, Malaya, Thailand, Indonesia and Burma. This was to be a prelude of the war effort of World War 11. Was it the late Meiji, late Edo "nativism" as well as "borrowed German racial theories" that had burst open into horrible life? Many decisions and wrong steps were taken." It was a hopelessly flawed chain of command, where thugs over-ruled their superior officers, junior officers in Tokyo, intimidated generals and Chiefs of Staff and pushed them around if not kicked them around, ordering and bullying civilian bureaucrats and pushing the Imperial Court to do their bidding." This is what can be said to be the essence of the powerful militarists and their prototypes later on, who persuaded the country to attack Pearl Harbor. They inflicted with such "zealous pride" to go on fighting a condemned war which was already seen to be a victory for the allies, but which served Japan's most honorable and best young men to die in a cause reawakening the former greatness of an Empire Japan had once held in the palms of its hand. The General of the Central China Area Army resigned his position, shaved his head and went into a Buddhist retreat. He was put into a court of trail for war criminals and told the Court that the massacre was a "national disgrace". However, he was executed and hanged. Yet many of the junior officers who had employed and given the orders went unpunished.

As the fighting continued, a maniacal Colonel Tsuji Masanota, who was often quoted for being the one held responsible for the outrage before the war's end in Soviet Russia. He wanted eastern Siberia. It was the wish of General Araki Sadao, Prince Konoe's education minister who most wanted to calm down his annoyance by purging Siberia and "clean it out like cleaning a room full of flies." Things by now looked so terrible that many thought war was inevitable. They considered striking north but those preferring to avoid a conflict with Soviet Russia went south. South East offered natural resources which they could control and allow the navy to building up it's strength for an eventual war in the Pacific. The Emperor himself preferred not all out war against Soviet Russia and given a choice preferred the navy side option. The situation was to make an agreement of settlement with Chiang Kai-shek and leave China, as well as cooperate with the West and give each other a handshake. At the same time they were "to prepare for all out war against the West, appoint a puppet Chinese regime in Nanking, get closer to Nazi Germany, strengthen all sides, for both army and navy and strike north or south and at the same time, let Tokyo 's dog wag it's tail once more in Manchuria." In1938, the fighting broke out in Korea, Manchukuo and the Soviet Union. The fighting between the Japanese and the Soviet troops started up at the Tumen River which was a Soviet fortress. Again the Soviet side had bombers and tanks whereas the Japanese side only had their "superior spirit" to guide them through the battles. After a fortnight, many had died on both sides, and though the Japanese side probably lost more than the Soviet side, the fighting brought no particular gain for either side. The Emperor had ordered all ceasefire and stop to the war. Colonel Tsuji ordered his men to carry on, deliberately disobeying his Emperor's Orders. About a year passed and in Outer Mongolia, the Japanese fought a useless battle though armed with "Molokov cocktails, sabers, guns and a few light tanks." They attacked GeneraL Zhukov's brigade of artillery and munitions, after which, they saw the slaughter of the dead corpses strewn everywhere in the flatlands where "vultures swooped down to make the corpses their feast". More than 20,000 soldiers died or of hunger, or thirst and deprivation was rampant with many falling because of sickness due to disease. The Russians kept up hostility and non-stop bombing. Colonel Tsuji was in fact promoted after this, and the plan to strike north was cancelled. The continuation in searching for their place in China was to look south, and to forget the north for a time to come.

CHAPTER 12

PEARL HARBOR
1941

The attack on Pearl Harbor took place on 7th December 1941. It was a day of great occasion for both the Japanese nation as well as for the Emperor Hirohito who dressed in his navy uniform in a wonderful frame of mind. It was an occasion to remember!

After this came the attacks on Singapore, the Dutch East Indies, the Philippines. This was "seisen" or the holy war for Asian "liberation" which could not have started off better.

It was the turning point of Japanese national feeling against the two great powers Britain and America. For the Japanese, the war started in a mood of celebration escalating into exalted sentiments of national pride which could only unify the country with aspirations of imminent victory and hope from worries they had known all too well. A war against China would have been considered an invasion. The transformation from war in the East to war in the West was thoroughly exhilarating giving them a sense of release from the burdensome worries they had previously experienced. The sentiment at the time gave over an official target of Japanese beliefs for a future liberalism in the sense of "individualism, pluralism, materialism, capitalism and democracy." In fact, Japan and Germany were of the same opinion or had the same ideas" Both acknowledged belief in their sense of racial purity as a main war-time propaganda." The Japanese had felt "snubs and slights" from the arrogant west and felt victims of themselves during the past years. Now, the Japanese were taken more seriously!

Before this, the conflicts in China made victims of their Asian partner. They accepted rather submissively the orders of their Japanese invaders. The Government was often unable to control the mutinies going on including coup d'etats in Tokyo! The Government now found a way of re-evaluating a program for a new Asian Order, at this point, and offered a new order based on "fraternal love, and cultural kinship, away from their attitude of governing an inferior state which ruled for and by "the sons of the divine empire."

Up until the War, Tokyo was already a westernized city. There were Hollywood movies, and classical and modern western music, as well as western books to read. This happened from the time of the Meiji Restoration up until 1941-1945. The Meiji Reformation involved pride and liberalism in the program to welcome the western way of life. However, Ian Buruma writes, "the Japanese war, was, among many other things, a war against liberalism." "Liberalism represented western thinking or westernization held by many shortly before and prior to the Pearl Harbor attack as the design for a stronger and united Asia under Tokyo." China had to be kept in place by stationing the military there. Japan knew they must penetrate deeper into Asia and in particular South East Asia where raw materials fuel and steel could supply their needs. They must find oil in the Dutch East Indies, as the Americans had stopped available sales of oil and scrap metal to the Japanese. The Japanese side realized they were over-come by "strangulation " of the ACDC powers, namely Britain, USA, Holland and China. It was General Tojo, who firstly controlled the extreme Imperial Way at a time when fascism was a way of controlling a revolution in hand. This was a national socialism or national revolution which took in the Nazi ideal of the revolution in hand, but Japan never based their war on a "fuhrer's diktat." It was a case of Germany's lead into the war which started an attack on the Soviet Union. By the time the Japanese military decided China must be positioned with the Japanese military, that Germany invaded France. In order to keep up their own self defense in matters related to the security and it's lifeline in the Pacific, Japan as a power in that region had to find resources such as oil, essential to the navy. Here one can understand how the Japanese clearly started "burning down bridges" as expressed here by their author. Because of the state of things left from the "China Incident" and its post war climate with Japan, the inevitability of war loomed over the negotiating tables between the countries. They knew that they could not afford to settle their differences peacefully on all occasions and abide by resolutions. This was the outstanding fact. They needed to take on South East Asia for oil supplies which led them to war. Uncertain about what to do, it became a waiting game and October would come and settle their long wait, as October was to be their deadline. It might bring together army and navy ministers of Japan who knew that the only way out could be signified by a system of kamikaze or diver bombers or Divine Wind, which had miraculously saved Japan from the Mongolian forces attacking their country. In 1274, the Japanese leaders as usual called for the Divine Wind to save the nation.

Nostalgically and quite truthfully said, the Japanese score to win true international acceptance after a severe defeat , opened the final question to the trade pioneered by Commodore Perry, "when Japan was still an economic pinnacle…can Japan finally bid the black ships farewell because they no longer need them". In his last phrase here, the author was alluding as well to a "change from an insular society to the old ways that no longer function."

CHAPTER 13

11 APRIL 1951

President Truman dismissed General McArthur for insubordination. This came as a shock to the Japanese, who revered and simply loved him as a Messiah who had worked hard for their country and their Emperor by re-constructing a new scheme to democratize and demilitarize Japan for the good.

" While many wonder at the renewal of government under the scrutiny of the allied forces, occupying Japan, it was confirmed in an American draft presented by Whitney to Matsumoto, who said to the latter that the Supreme Commander had been unyielding to the defense of the Emperor against mounting pressure from the outside to render him a subject of criminal investigation. He had thus defended the Emperor because he considered that this was the cause of right and justice, and would continue along that course to the end of his ability. But, gentlemen, the Supreme Commander is not omnipotent. He feels, however that acceptance of the provisions of this new Constitution would render the Emperor practically unassailable, He feels it would bring much closer the day of your freedom from control by the Allied Powers, and that it would provide your people with the essential freedoms which the Allied Powers demand on this belief."

At the appointment of Prime Minister Yoshida, Whitney and other Americans doubted the new government's appointment as anything other than one that was reactionary and hostile. There was unhappiness amongst the Japanese at the course the Occupation was taking was slower than they would have liked. Though the Constitution was to be revised for changing the practical law of government, and did do all "to preserve the throne", it was a time of transition from one government to the other with all speed to obtain an earlier settlement to forward a quicker end of the Occupation. Time was a factor of importance as little would they have known it would take more than a decade of

American presence to finish the war and see it set on a different course for the vanquished nation.

MacArthur gained momentum as he presided in an "imperial style" allowing his subordinates to work around him while he guided the course and the way he wanted the new Constitution to be written and acted upon. This was to be a mark of history of the time. Essentially, he had respect for Japan always viewing the Emperor as "the head of state". Those working for him were young men who would "accord to the simile that the Emperor was the symbol of the state and the unity of the people." Kades and his men explained that "sovereignty" rested entirely with the people and this was a concept considered revolutionary! The Supreme Commander pushed hard to render a "liberalist theme" to cooperate with "the feudal system of Japan" which must cease to a certain extent, while providing at the same time a guarantee that the representative government would bring about a "broad range of civil liberties and human rights." Oddly enough, this section of the rights and duties of the people was taken then as now, as the basic ground for the " most liberal guarantee of human rights in the world."

The renunciation of the war clause was toned down a lot so that it read: "war as a sovereign right of the nation is abolished." It continued that "the threat or use of force is forever renounced as a means for settling disputes with any other nation." The part two of the clause makes a gesture to say that there would be an allowance for "modest rearmament" for the sake of preserving its own security." This left the "seed of decades of controversy." Even now, in 2009, Japan have a right to defend itself through the Self Defense Forces allowed to them by the United Nations. This was in agreement with the question of Japan's military power to return or not to return. The heroic Yukio Mishima, in the early 1970's tried to persuade the government of Japan, unsuccessfully to bring Japan back to a military rule and style of government as in the days before the post defeat. We are told about his disgrace at not winning over his attempt to overthrow the Pacifists and American Constitutional founders for the New Japan, which forced him to commit hara kiri or ritual suicide!

At the same time, the Japanese war crimes tribunals were being heard under the Kellogg - Briand Pact, of 1928, which viewed war crimes, as the "violations of it's principles emerging at that very time…
"While their Pact offered peace, it became a "double edged sword,"

used in the new drafted constitution, protecting the Emperor while at the same time, the officers and officials were "cut down". This seems unfair but they served to die for their state and the Emperor at all times, until the end.

The "model" Constitution as composed for the charter for the new Diet, head of Government, was to be taken and accepted as such for a guideline to practice along the lines of their newly formed Constitution. On February 10th General Whitney transmitted the draft of a new constitution to the Supreme Allied Commander. He pointed out that this new draft was considered the "collective view of Government Section" which represented every "form of American political thought" and had been written "after taking the historical development of the Japanese Constitution into consideration and giving attention to American and European principles". However, the Japanese Government would accept it and obviously amend it according to their Will, which would be reviewed as and when they needed to re-think again over the strategies. Whitney said as a matter of fact "it constitutes a sharp swing from the extreme right in political thinking-yet yields nothing to the radical concept of the extreme left."

MacArthur in a sweeping gesture made a single change to it. He eliminated restrictions on amending the "bill of human rights". General MacArthur had been reinstated in the Far East since the end of the War in 1945. He had been responsible for insuring another disastrous World War. The Occupation was terminated and a peace treaty was in hand for all 48 nations to sign apart from the Soviet Union which could not settle peace on account of a confirmed dispute regarding the islands north of Hokkaido.

Although Japan asked for "overall peace" together with their newly agreed attitude, this peace could not be considered due to the "ferocious cold war atmosphere of the time." The grand ceremony opening the Treaty to be signed took place in September 1951. The concession the American made realized the forwarding of another treaty signed, at the same time regarding China and Taiwan in which stipulation had to agree that isolationism and economic containment was partial to the rules set for the Chinese. This was a stern measure, shocking Tokyo. On the other hand, the Japan-US Security Treaty forced Japan to agree on the American extraterritorial claims or rights for a military presence and installation, which nobody had so far bargained for. As the writer says, the NY Times at the same time said of this period in Japan, the inauguration proved to be a period when "Japan is free, yet not free." Sovereignty was restored on 28th April 1952. This embarked on giving the nation at large a role of "subordinate independence" which is never quite the same as full independence. The strategy for this allowed greater security in a dangerous world for the likes of a country considered at risk. This may be viewed like a medical assessment of a nation suffering mental dis-order! It would be a presumption to suggest this as a whole sweeping statement against any individual state or nation without sitting in a court room held on an accusation of libel and slander. This could be reversed on a vice-versa tone. The realization of such a statement is often undone by a method of treating a subject from the nation concerned and detained for however long it takes them to be satisfied with that state. One can perceive there from a medical eye view a certain disdain or if you like," prejudicial thought "which come out eventually in the open as an undeclared war against the sovereignty of a nation or state. The conclusions drawn are usually of a financial sort. It brings about devastation as any modern conflict would return. Bearing in mind the global financial or fiscal conflicts, it must be true to some extent to say the above. The medical analysis is all that would seem to account for much of this inglorious war against the world economy. After all, one guesses that it was done for the conflicts of the world for psychiatrists and their paramedics. It is to ask about this to see more clearly the understated conflict of Mishima, before his death in the 1970's. Possibly the old enemy from somewhere in the western hemisphere proved to be constipation-as relative to the psychiatric treatment in hand in another part of the world. This is history and not meant as anything other than a historic fact, whether one understands it or not. Now many years later, the new belief is in better health and next to this, is the health of the economy. We put out trust in health and invest in it. We just as equally put our money into things identified as self maintenance themes, and this is the norm for a better and healthier economy. We never confuse health issues with financial health and or wealth, but this in light of the present day conflicts may no longer be true. Indeed one ties in with the other to a degree? There are financiers in the world who are more suited and experienced then medical practitioners about financial matters. The latter have the professionalism and experience of medical things and problems they sort out. We pay them as we, must pay interest charges to the bank and advisers who are there to talk to us and help if and when they can. Medical insurance is another way of honoring the medical teams and groups who are always there to help out. Given too much money by the Government to the hospitals could swing the other way around where the power would go to none other than the hospitals and therefore the medicals. This is not what is meant by seeking to restore the world financially as the most able to cure just about everything. Some mean to give more power to them by the misappropriated idea of resolving a growing problem in both mental health hygiene as well as physical illness. Paying the doctors and taking out medical insurance, safeguarding and protecting oneself and taking care of oneself can only help pave the way for better recovery. These effects are completely normal and medical. The doctors have taught everyone this much if not much more. We must remember and next time around, pay attention to their wise words in self help and self care.

It is obvious that for sometime I have been warred on and for this reason, in a smaller capacity, I decided to write the book I am writing about the Pacific War of the Second World War. I have my remembrances too of the dead though I speak of the dead of this year rather than 65 years ago. To conclude, both sides saw their falls, but the side that lost the most must have been mine. The point I make is the potential killer threat lurking behind the scenes prepared to pounce like a Black Panther terrorist to kill one way or the other. It is, as somebody said the other day, "primeval instinct" which has instigated the problem of near death misses. The word is economy and this sounds out the real reasons for this obtrusive and distasteful conduct. The resolution here is to call an amnesty of sorts – a type of armistice day. A negotiation to quell the uprisings by their terrorists sexists, out for blood. This should be the call to stop this militant style attack on innocent people while they sleep. Let me explain. If I shall not get back my friends then I could lose my money. Many people as the world knows, have lost a lot of money and some have even gone bankrupt. Many live by now in fear of losing more money. Trade is impossible, shops are left empty. This must clearly advertise the problems the government have given one and all. Good economy is like a golden ray in the sky .Which one will it save? Unfair systems lock us in, and no real justice is available to any to help because of a drug problem such as dependence on it or a money worry which has struck all in society from the bottom to the top. Heterosexual rights are only for a few women lucky enough not to have been singled out by their gays. It is not a time of politeness or the entente cordiale so famous in the days of a different time. Their game is sick and vicious. They treat as if we are all a public convenience for them. Nobody bats an eye lid and nobody says anything. This is some of the goings on. It seems many will have lost futures for the sake of a few fashionable prostitutes. One hangs on nervously wondering when things will get back to normal and until then just hold on tight!

It is internal city conflicts of a potential civil war, a war that had commenced sometime ago and by now has declared itself more openly. Like all wars, it is insane. Many die by night and often blameless innocent children unfortunately. This is the drug war. At the end we all agree that we feel the economic pinch which we had not felt before, and I think this is a global effect rather than just an individual one. The credit crunch has hit all of us very hard.

I now continue the Japanese history of the liberalization of Japan after the American Occupation.

The new status gained gave rise to "liberalism and demilitarization and democracy" which did not allow Japan to be a part of the "pax Americana" which did effect criticism from the government and community as well as from the media and literati.

CHAPTER 14

1948

Kishi Nobusuke, a war crime suspect was released from Sugamo prison at Christmas time in 1948. He had once been under General Tojo as the minister of commerce and industry, when Pearl Harbor took place. It is a wonder how this man was to be the President of Japan ten years later and would make history as the outspoken Chosu man who belonged to the provincial samurai ancestry a zealous right wing of Japanese political life. He stood on the opposite pole to the liberalists. Another cell mate of his was Sasakawa Ryoichi , who had once been a leader of a facist party in the 1930's, had been a notorious racqueteer in Occupied China and was brilliant when it came to war time connections for "shady money". Not only was he a "formidable backroom operator" with connections with the postwar conservative politicians but he was released on the same day as Kishi from Sugamo prison. Another connection and friend was Yoshiuda Shigeru, who was in charge in 1948, and who also moved in the same high political circles as the other two. However, they did not get along with each other very well. In fact, they disliked each other. Yoshida and Tosa belonged to the People's Rights Movement and was a conservative. Yoshida once called a socialist Member of Parliament "a damned fool" in front of an open Diet. Kishi was always on the side of the extreme right Conservative wing. In Manchukuo, he worked for General Tojo, and the Kwangtung army, and by 1939, he was in favor of Nazi Germany and strengthened his ties with them. He sided with the military rather than with businessmen, and while in prison, believed in the "just war" Japan had just fought! Kishi was a defender of democracy after the war. He was "authoritarian, nationalistic and socialistic" planning an economy to bolster up the nation and planned to spread wealth. He was opposed to a "laissez-faire" system or a liberal Anglo Saxon capitalism. He wanted a centralized industrial planning that had to be carefully worked out, very similar to the Russian five-year plan. He met a former Nazi economist minister, a Hyalmar Schacht, while on a visit to Germany. Kishi's economic ideas would always remain a fixed ideology especially amongst Japanese thinkers and others whose thoughts were aligned to their way of thinking.

In 1951, MacArthur was on his way out of Japan, and John Foster Dulles was on his way in to Tokyo for a peace treaty. MacArthur reigned supreme during the post-war years, and tried to build a national Japan into the "Switzerland of the Pacific". However, in 1959, the Korean War broke out and changed this. Japan's Pacifist policy remained intact though they were recruited by the Americans to police the state dressed in second hand uniforms and even given "machine guns, bazookas and tanks!" Yoshida referred to them as Imperial Army veterans and not real soldiers. They worked to crack down on communist agitators which proved an American offensive over these Occupation years. They were later renamed the Japanese Defense Forces which was a type of self defense force. They still survive today as Japan's only right in military deployment. The Americans had agreed to give over military security for them in the Pacific and based their military base in Okinawa where they still apply the security for the entire nation.

To continue this I can explain how John Foster Dulles demanded 350,000 Japanese men in arms. Yoshida thought it was a breach of the peace constitution. It was too much of an imposition or threat and he staged a protest against him with 75,000 Japanese Defense Forces which improved his claim. Though he offered Japanese territory to the American for army bases to be stationed in Okinawa, for the purpose of installing a US Government administration there, he was not fully in accord with a long term contract for this arrangement. Though the Americans would be there to provide national security to the small nation of Japan in Okinawa, with the "Yoshida Deal" Japan would retain it's legitimate sovereignty to a point and the American security would provide the security Japan needed. In a peace treaty, the security treaty was signed simultaneously on December 15 1951 in San Francisco. The "Yoshida Deal" had been accomplished.

Although Yoshida's deal was done, there was a lot of protest and disagreement by the Left and by 22 May 1958, the crowds staging the protest went as far as charging the Police on the Imperial Palace Plaza. This was retaliation and general unrest that "guns, tear gas and batons" were used against the crowd. The Leftists had "stars in their eyes" for the Soviet Union and felt remorse and guilt for the loss of Chinese Communists. They wanted to cancel the security arrangements with the US. They wanted to be back amongst their own Asian neighbors promising they would never war on them again. In the meanwhile, the Diet were revising the Constitution as set out by General Macrthur, and during the time it took to do this, there were many protests and uprisings against this controversial security.

The 1950's however began the string of famous productions of Japanese movies under the directorship of "Ozu, Mizoguchi and Kurosawa."

Hiroshima and Nagasaki were never to be forgotten and became the symbol for anti-American Pacificism-the Japanese Left refused to play down Japanese war crimes, insisting in the 1950s's and discussed this more critically and analytically than the Germans in Germany.

General MacArthur had been the Allied Supreme Commander since September1946 and by May 1951, he had reached the age of 71. During his time, he was much loved, revered and a national monument to the people of Japan, who considered him little else than their Messiah who had restored them back to a life and a country they felt happy in. He was for them a part of the Japanese heritage and a leader comparable to Christ giving a sermon on the Mount. He had delivered them out of their grief and suffering from the days immediately after the end of the World War. He was the Buddha- like "friend from afar", sanctified for liberating Japan out of the nightmarish war conditions. He was thanked for giving hope to the Japanese people and gave over to them a happiness endowed with security and peace to brush away their fears at the prospect of the occupation of an alien force and former enemy. As simple as it sounds, it has been told how the Japanese people confessed their worst sins to him as if he was their confessor. They "unburdened" themselves of their worst fears as well as hopes treating him as their psychiatrist or next best friend. In fact, MacArthur never betrayed Japan and along the way received recognition and amazing friendliness by the people who believed he was "their godly and divine miracle maker and savior." Many gifts were bestowed on him, a list so long; I could not recount them all in this little book.

In 1948, for instance, a fisherman gave him fat fishes caught locally with a sincere and very simple faith in the American who had made it possible for the Japanese to achieve" what could not have been attained even in many years of bloody struggle". Gifts and gift giving is a national practice bestowed to the benefactor or superior. It is something that is the way of life for all people in Japan, and not considered anything other than a formality and gesture of good will and respect. The people of Japan are sensitive to good manners and are famous for their politeness.

"Another gave him a beautiful brocade kimono which took him three years to create. The brocade had 70 million stitches and he hid himself in seclusion in a Kyoto shrine to make the masterpiece of the era. The gift was accompanied by a Shinto prayer and offered to the general as a "symbol of our 70 million people-each stitch representing one living Japanese".

A beggar recruited himself to a bakery, to ask permission to bake a birthday cake for him. His request was accepted.

Some aborigines even sent him the hide of a deer which they had slain especially to present him with together with antlers. They expressed their "token of respect" to the General who had "secured land for our people and given Japan a democratic society, based on law and order."

The 1950's displayed the dire consequences of the return to Communism which led to Marxist dogma, and a few accepted the Chinese communists were no better than freedom fighters over Japanese Capitalist Imperialists "surrendering to the Emperor system". The new enemy cited and rediscovered was American Imperialism and its "Japanese running dogs"

Kishi and the Right always maintained the war had been a just war. The Left claimed it a barbarity, the Right felt they had done nothing wrong in particular no different from other nations involved in the conflict. There was controversy and to this day, the Teachers Union and the Conservative Ministry of Education fight on about it. Whatever aspect the mind seeks, it is true to say what Richard Nixon admitted in Article 9 in 1953 " it was an honest mistake". Regardless, the war, as seen in the Japanese press, adheres to historians who stick to the academics of historical and factual events of this past Great War. In the meanwhile, Communism eventually became less popular, and after the 1953 riots, members in the Diet held a smaller marginal seat in the

Lower House. However, the Socialists were backed up by large trade unions. The Democratic and Liberal Party was led by Yoshida.

In 1955, the Socialist Party outnumbered many in the House, and at one point, it appeared they stood a chance of winning. The right and left wings merged into one party and called themselves the Japanese Socialist Party (JSP). This opened a forum to merge the Democrats with the Liberals which had extraordinary effect and again was led by Kishi. This was Big Business that was the striking force building up to this moment. The first LDP leader was chosen a Hatoyama, another veteran of the "kokusai elite." The purge of alignments was called the "1955 System." Soon after the LDP System over the 1955 System became a takeover for the entire control over the Socialists aspirations to become the model for the "workers Revolution in Asia". The LDP were funded not only by money from construction companies, industrial corporations, CIA slush funds and trading companies but from big business, Washington and senior bureaucrats. They were well rewarded with the constant flow of money into their constituencies. The Socialists never had the chance again to govern for forty years. Even after this time, they did not last long and never returned having won back full recovery of political status.

CHAPTER 15

TANAKA

This famous well known politician distributed to Japanese politicians and collected from Lockheed Corporation, cash in exchange for an aircraft deal. It was a story of renowned controversy about Kodama Yoshio, another wartime criminal who had been imprisoned with Kishi Nobusuke. This led to a young porno movie actor dressing up in uniform, crashing his light aircraft straight into the Lockheed Office in Tokyo. He wore the Kamikaze uniform. He acted against capitalist corruption. His last words were "Long Live the Emperor." His contemporaries understood him to be a tragic but equally fanatical person under the circumstances.

Tanaka was regarded by the Japanese press as the politician with "money politics". He never stopped "constructing roads, bridges, airports, conference centers, pachinko parlors, more museums, more theme parks and industrial zones." Many were useful, but at the same time were unnecessary. Japan's wealth was greater but there was much corruption at the same time. He was a man operating in scandalous proportions by way of his corruption and usage of great amounts of money to pass to other politicians in the wake of his period in office. His great rival was Fukuda Takeo, who like Kishi Nobusuke, started his career in Manchuria. He wanted to bring down Mr Tanaka and have him thrown out of the LDP System which Tanaka had all but usurped. However Fukuda could not overthrow his rival. Tanaka became an independent lawmaker years after the Lockheed scandal. He even controlled the very heart of the LDP massive system! His was the Ikeda deal and the 70's money politics. "He was neither ever a Democratic Reformer, just manipulating the system to create more wealth and jobs for the greater majority of people. Tanaka was formerly a construction man. It was construction that funded his career in politics. He married the daughter of his construction boss. It is said that during his years in office, he never lost sight of the wealth created which seemed "the Japanese bonanza would never end." By the 1980s, a marked intellectual support group began to complain about the lack of values in modern Japan.

Another President by the name of Nakasone Yasuhiro in the 1980's tried his mark by promoting the old nationalism of the Imperial Institution buying back the uniqueness of the Japanese spirit.

After this, when Koizumi Jumichiro came into office, he promised reforms of abolishing party faction and controlling a better bureaucratic system, Koizumi had been a media star in 2001, and many had hoped, with his young bright appearances together with his promises of reform, that he might turn out to be a Gorbachev type leader-the reformer who brought down the system. Presently as then in the days of Koizumi, Japan's frustrated nationalism and economic despair has proved that the country was on a down-hill slide into a "non-directed policy and way of life."

However in spite of Kishi who had tried to buy down Mr Tanaka, and his system, it was, nonetheless a time of great economy both stable and futuristic. Businesses cooperated "against virtues of obedience, self sacrifice, working nationalists upholding true characteristics". Technicians and their dexterity, superior sensitivity, group consciousness - this was the past war boom that had smoothly gone from war time kokutai to the LDP system. We are not permitted to forget either that the post war boom had both Japanese as well as American fathers! Kishi was working on a resolution to restore back to the Constitution a resolution which had to restore back to Japan its independence as a sovereign power. A new treaty had to be revised in order to amend the constitution and the security.

The marked interest of Japanese government policies and politica sometimes coincided with demonstrations against them by Japanese who struggled to identify themselves as their own self ruling sovereign state. In one incident when further arms embargos were brought to the shores of their military bases, a protest broke out and a young girl was caught in the stampede that occurred and was killed. After this a demonstration broke out with jargons and angry protests saying "Yankee, go home." Japan's only stability was to keep a Self Defense Force, which is all they had left to them in effect for world conflicts.

The Socialist, no doubt, always in revolt called against "American Imperialism" the common enemy of the Japanese and Chinese peoples."

Eisenhower's visit to Tokyo had to be cancelled. It almost looked like a Revolution on the horizon. All the old mistrust and hatred of Americans reinforced and gathered menacingly in the open streets. Kishi no doubt thought of deploying the Self Defense forces, but he did not carry this out.

1960, the same disagreeable reaction returned, but this time in the Diet. The Socialists took the Diet Speaker and locked him up. General Tojo's Defense Counsel at the Tokyo War Crimes Tribunal ordered riot police to come and release him immediately! After midnight the Treaty went ahead without a Japanese member at all. Kishi had gone ahead and done it. He had to resign quickly. An assassination was planned to kill him. His formidable career after the war had brought him to be a past master at avoiding open conflict and he went out of public life however dealing as a great puppet player!

After Kishi, came Ikeda Hayato, who never resolved the Constitution problem. However time passed leading Japan into a great economic power which survived all other interests. Tokyo built their own Eiffel Tower, and by 1964, had constructed the first bullet train speeding between Tokyo and Osaka in less than four hours. The world arrived for the Olympic Games. The Japanese felt peace with themselves and for good reasons.

After Kishi came his protégé, Sato Eisaku, Kishi's younger brother. Historically, he said that when Japan went against America, Japan suffered. His policy was admirable…"my policy therefore was to cooperate fully with the US to ensure peace in the world." Sato promised peace, and more peace. He won the Nobel Peace Prize in 1972.

Japan, from the days of World War conflict to the days of the Imperial state was always a mark of "longevity and timeless transition of that Imperial state of democracy." This was "peace as in war" and this was symbolic of the "unity of the people" for the subjects of Japan would regard Emperor s Hirohito's death in 1989 as the "signal of an end of an era – the Showa period was over and the calendars must be changed."

What has marked this end is the unusual aspect of the end of the cold war as depicted by the falling down of the Berlin Wall. This marked the time limit proving Japan had caught up with the West in all things related to the economy and technology as well as the "vision and flexibility" for charting out a new course. The days of his august reign were over. His death as related before put his heir and his son Crown Prince Akihito on the throne.

CHAPTER 16

AFTER KOIZUMI

Now, after Koizumi, a new man appeared on the Tokyo map, being Ishihara Shintaro, a man to watch for. Ishihara made his name as a popular novelist in the 1950's.He was outspoken, his views were generally broadcast, advertised, and made into books and video recordings. They are seen as well in T.V. and talk shows. Like others before him, he had emphasized his dis-like of the bureaucracy of the LDP system. He felt that Japan's insipid and defeatist advertisements divided the nation of better policies. He believed the war was his predecessor's war but Japan should cut off the "umbilical cord" with Washington and respond to the calls of the powers of Asia. He sought to live in a less colonialised American style Japan and return to the older Asian way talking more closely and more often to his Asian neighbors. Japan may still be reaction to the defeat of their past war which gave an infantile type dependency on the US on all matters. However, he felt these problems could be resolved in the years much after the post surrender defeat of his country.

However obvious it was, there would be serious consequences if the U.S. should completely withdraw from Japan. The conflicts may re-commence with Korea and it's arsenals, as well as the threat of open armaments gathered in Taipei and how China might divulge themselves into a nuclear state ready to champion the rest of Asia. The stability could go once and for all, regardless of how Tokyo may feel about the many years of established security in Japan for Japan. It is almost like an ill advised divorce! It could be the worst threat on peace and security nationally as well as an economic tragedy. Some continued to argue.

CHAPTER 17

HIROSHIMA AND NAGASAKI AS WRITTEN AT THE UNITED NATIONS, NEW YORK CITY,UNITED STATES

1945 was the year that ended World War 11. It was to see a devastating nuclear attack on the Empire of Japan by the US, under President Harry Truman on August 6th and 9th 1945. Six months passed with intense fire bombing on Japanese cities until the nuclear bomb "Little Boy" dropped on Hiroshima.

This first attack occurred on 6th August, followed on 9th August by "The Fat Boy" a nuclear bomb dropped on Nagasaki. These are the only two attacks ever delivered with nuclear weapons in the history of warfare.

The majority hit civilians. The main part of the devastation took 140,000 people killed in Hiroshima alone, with another 80,000 dead in Nagasaki. Since then, many more died from injuries or illness attributed to radiation exposure.

It took six more days after, for Japan's final surrender on 2nd September, officially ending the Pacific War and therefore World War 11. Germany signed it's surrender on 7th May, ending the war in Europe. The bombings led Japan into the Agreement to be non-participants in non-nuclear projects, forbidding this nation from nuclear arms.

Years later, on 6th August, 1952, a memorial cenotaph was erected. Under the cenotaph, which is in the shape of an ancient clay house, rests a store coffin. On it are inscribed the words "Rest in Peace, for the mistake shall not be repeated. "As of 6th August 1980, the death registers every year after stands at 98,685, less than half of the estimated 200,000 or more who died when the A-bomb exploded on Hiroshima.

On Nagasaki only half the dead have been identified. It has been a custom to hold the peace memorial ceremony by hanging a big curtain in front of the Statue. The design of the flowers placed in front of the statue, represents pigeons with their wings outstretched toward the sun. They represent the figure appealing for eternal world peace as well as consoling the souls of the dead.

The A-bomb did not only injure the masses, but it destroyed buildings. It destroyed all the living and the community of the living. The experience of Hiroshima and Nagasaki is not confined solely to war damage. It represents genocide "the obliteration of the society" and devastation of the environment. It is the first experience in the history of mankind which "augurs the destruction of the earth."

According to a report by the U.N. Secretary General, in the autumn of 1980, there are 40,000-50,000 nuclear weapons stocked in the world today, a number equivalent to one million Hiroshima type A-bombs.

This would mean, the present nuclear arsenal stocked today is enough to mass murder the entire population of the earth several dozen times. Nuclear weapons as this could threaten mankind and hold them in a state between survival and eradication".

It is said that the world lives in an age of nuclear horror whether we accept it or not. In order to better secure and ensure the perpetration of mankind, we must abolish all nuclear weapons from earth. "Japan is in the forefront of this drive for peace."

The "Stockholm Appeal" of 1950, started a movement against nuclear weapons. When the A-bombs were used to threaten the Korean War, which broke out in June of that year, "the Appeal was promoted world-wide and 500 million signatories were collected." When a hydrogen bomb test was carried out at Bikini A toll on 1st March 1954, a Japanese tuna fishing vessel "Fukuruyu Maru No 5" was suddenly covered in "deadly ashes" and Mr Aikichi Kuboyama, a crew member, died due to radiation.

This effectively triggered a signature collection movement against atomic and hydrogen bombs all over Japan. 30 million signatures were collected that year (1954). This powerful message brought into play a First World Conference against A&H Bombs, which was held the following year in August 1955.

After this, a global movement demanding the end of nuclear weapons was organized calling itself the NGO and by the non-aligned neutral countries, which comprises two thirds of the countries in the world. The NGO is an organization formed on Clause 71 of the UN Charter, which vigorously impeaches the competition for nuclear development by holding the Hiroshima International Forum commemorating the 30th anniversary of the Atomic Bombing in Tokyo , Hiroshima ,Nagasaki, done in the summer of 1977, the NGO holds itself as a way to protect mankind from another nuclear crisis.

A global event was noted by the UN Special session on Disarmament, held for the first time from May 23-July 1, 1978. This important proposal of non-aligned nations in front of the General Assembly took place in 1976. Important resolutions were made in terms of disarmament, including the non-use of nuclear weapons. The participation of 35 nuclear and non-nuclear countries was to be formed. The week of October 24 each year was designated from then on as the "U.N. Disarmament week" – a time when each country would emphasize the cause for a settled disarmament.

At the 33rd session of the U.N. General Assembly meeting held in the autumn of 1976, the following "recommendations" was made after the "Special Session." These were the following: 1) the use of nuclear weapons violated the U.N. Charter.2) the international agreement was to protect non-nuclear countries.3) nuclear weapons must not be deployed against non-nuclear countries.4) nuclear tests must not be conducted. 5) an investigation must be made to terminate the use and production of nuclear weapons and it's testing equipment,

The above recommendations have not been fully carried out. It is important and necessary to mobilize public opinion world-wide in order to strive more peacefully to strengthen the second U.N. Special Session on Disarmament to be held in 1982.

At the end of this passage, the writer says "the devil's weapon made by man must be removed by the wisdom of man. We must strengthen our belief with another and define what we can do now" and what we cannot fail at. They believe in a gathering of effort to unite a force to abolish all nuclear weapons in order to secure "eternal survival, prosperity and peace for all mankind".

CHAPTER 18

PRESIDENT JOHN F. KENNEDY

Many Presidents of the United States talked of arms and during those years they attributed much of their talk to nuclear disarmament. This continues today.

President Kennedy demonstrated on more than one occasion that his belief was to control nuclear arms and disband the use of arms as a force to use against other countries for war.

One mentions that present day nuclear problems re-rises giving birth to other countries such as IRAN and North Korea as nuclear bound states holding nuclear arms. Countries trying to control or eliminate the use of these arms are finding trouble doing this as often, negotiations and peace talks are not always possible; in the case of North Korea, no open talks are invited in; in the case of Iran, the confusion over the elections has stalled talks until the decision has been made by the true leader to invite others to discuss this.

The old theme of "mentalite" returns again this time about peace keeping movements in the world at large, rather than the precursor to this word, in a world movement of only Asian countries and Empire Builders. We speak of President Kennedy for instance and his summary of July 1963 when he said; "some say it is useless to speak of world peace or world law or world disarmament…that it will be useless until the leaders of the Soviet Union adopt a more enlightened attitude. Our attitude is as essential as theirs." He continued saying "Let us examine our attitude, toward the Soviet Union. We find Communism profoundly repugnant as a negation of personal freedom and dignity. But we can still hail the Russian people for their many achievement –in science and in space…world peace, like community peace, does not require that each man love his neighbor-it requires only that they live together in mutual tolerance, submitting their disputes to just and peaceful settlement. "At a May meeting, the Senate called for a Resolution banning "all tests that contaminate the atmosphere."

May 17th 1963

He compares a weapon which is two or three times more explosive than the bombs that destroyed Hiroshima and Nagasaki. He said in his own words "I am haunted by this". He believed nuclear proliferation was the single biggest problem of the 1960's and the most compelling reason for a test ban…to prevent Communist China from developing a bomb. Many Americans did not know the current feelings amongst the other nations about the bomb which they considered "an icon of national adulthood." He had a battle on from the beginning about nuclear disarmament.

The President not only had problems with Cuba during the Cuban missile crisis but was up to his neck with a war on in Vietnam. On 26th July, an eyewitness sent a report to Washington "delivering an alarm signal to the White House". They read how a ship named "Mariaillanova" had entered the Cuban port armed with 500 generals on board and unloading technicians who started unloading baggage and cargoes…The Captain of the ship stopped over in New Orleans and reported to the US navy officials, they had seen a 5000 ton Russian ship carrying about 2000 men in uniform. Furthermore, on the 5th August, he was quoted saying that going through Matanzas," I saw between 250-300 men, foreigners, standing near parked trucks near the Penas Altas bar. "This was closed. Then a McClone, one of Kennedy's men was the only eyewitness who was left in little doubt that there were surface-to-air missiles in the trucks called "SA-2S" and he guessed they were to be used as "coastal defense weapons". It goes on to say that McClone realized and guessed by the size and style of the weapons, that they were probably a category of SAMS-ballistic missiles which in turn had a 90 mile range to the USA with MRBMS ranges that could reach Miami and IRBMS which could reach 1500 miles and even hit Washington from Cuba. "It is more than likely that Castro had been shopping around for defense weapons to retaliate against invasion on his own territory of Cuba, and he had hit a deal with Kruschev.

Not since World War 11 had there been so many models of nuclear arms. There was land-and-submarine fired missiles; Polaris submarine missiles, which when detonated could carry out a devastation worse than Hiroshima or Nagasaki .

In the meanwhile, the Soviets had built up a strong arsenal of weapons in the event they needed these weapons to return fire if fired upon by the United States. So they had weapons installed in Cuba which carried a radius of 90 miles which could destroy Florida. The United States, were, under the circumstances in a position of considerable vulnerability against a hostile and immediate attack, which had been spotted by accident!.

Further investigation using U-2 spy planes and reconnaissance technology, proved that this was matched by evidence and "ground" and aerial photographs had been taken. However, the cautious investigation which followed to find out as much as possible about the weapons being installed, aggravated the situation in America whereby a Republican Senator, a Kenneth Keating stood up on the floor and attacked the White House. He said angrily that the approach was "too calm and reaction to the evidence of Communist infiltration 90 miles away" was much too lacking in the way it was being handled. The Americans stood to lose their security if the situation did not improve and he felt too that the President should call for arms to retaliate against the Communists in Cuba. He also went on to say that the Americans would quickly lose their faith in him and that he must decide more quickly and promptly in order to safeguard measures to assure the nation that it was taken care of and there was no imminent threat or danger to themselves or their country. Kennedy knew all too well that this was going to be his greatest "political problem."

Somebody I once knew said and I quote her "he is timide" in the French sense rather than in the English word "timid". By this they meant he was a quiet man prone to thought before acting on a challenge. He was thoughtful or "cautious".

Keating, in the meanwhile, asked a lot of questions which went unanswered many times. This caused great embarrassment to the White House Officials. There were no further answers either to reply to questions such as "what are they going to build with the new equipment" or "what will the army of technicians be required to maintain? The "true story" behind the Soviet Occupation of Cuba with weapons was really enough to blow the top off things. They thought the President too soft on Communism a "taboo in US policy at the time.

The press said of him in a 3rd September article "Kennedy..is caught between Cuban charges that he is planning to invade the island and mounting Congressional demands that he should do precisely this."He was subsequently renamed "The do-nothing President." At a meeting with Robert Kennedy, the Soviet Ambassador, a man named Anatol Dobrynin told him that he had defensive objectives in Cuba.

Kruschev sent a dispatch to the Soviet Embassy with a personal guarantee that he would do nothing to upset "internal political affairs", or aggravate tension in the relationships between our two countries. He only wanted to remind the President of his wish to discuss a peace settlement in Germany and West Berlin…"Although the charges never stopped and Keating's forceful voice demanded the over-throw of the Soviets and their weapons in Cuba, there was no sign of resignation to give in to his request and Kennedy kept up his determination "to watch, wait and see policy". As a result, McGeorge Bundy , a President's man, wrote down in his memo of 13th September news conference…"the immediate hazard is that the Administration may appear to be weak and indecisive…"

A 12th September news headline, read this; "Rockets will Blast the US if it invades Cuba."Regardless, the President and his entourage of men refused to move from their position. He held a news conference and said this; "I would like to take this opportunity to set the matter in perspective…it is Mr Castro and his supporters who are in trouble… he should try to arouse the Cuban people by charges against an imminent American invasion…these new shipments do not constitute a threat to any other part of the hemisphere…I have indicated that if Cuba should possess a capacity to carry out offensive actions against the US, that the US would act…"Unlike the Democrats, the Republicans were fighting hard for a war against Cuba. Keating undisputedly made Kennedy suffer stress and tension by his overwhelming contest against him in the run up to the elections. His "get tough on Castro stance" was enough to make 51% of the majority believe that an assail on Cuba might lead the country to World War11 again. So drastic was the agreement that Kennedy's go slow method and option not to war on Cuba, met with continued disapproval from the Senate, and Adlai Stevenson, his envoy at the United Nations overheard the President says his worst fear:" it's Pearl Harbor in reverse." The British Ambassador, Ormsby-Gore felt Americans "over-reacted" and voted for a "blockade" rather than bombing. However, the official message, he sent back to London to the Prime Minister, then Harold MacMillan was the warning "of an impending crisis."

By 22 October, the President knew that due to the Cuban crisis, they had lost their election and at the same time, the US was on national high alert with a strike about to be requested before Congress and sanction to use military force at the UN headquarters in NY. The President wrote in his notebook that by now he had justification to act with hostility against Cuba by the "will and act of US self defense". One remembers how the Joint Chiefs of Staff, Bundy, Acheson and Taylor by now urged the President to act for all out air-strike against Cuba. There had been strikes on the Bay of Pigs in Cuba in the recent past, but the mission however changed, and became one of importance when it was apparent that the known Soviet missiles must be destroyed. Total destruction, they realized would be impossible, blockading rather than give in to a bombing campaign was the resolve of Robert Kennedy, for if they should proceed with a bombing campaign, they might be forced to give up their military bases in Turkey and Italy where their Jupiters were stored. Though the arguments of the pros and cons for the blockade ran a mile, it was the threat from the Republicans that the President offered a brief statement…"the transformation of Cuba into a Communist base of operation , a few minutes from our coast, by jet planes, missiles or sub-marines , is an incredibly dangerous development to have been permitted by our Republican policy makers." Diplomatically, Adlai Stevenson, though a good friend of Jackie, the President's wife, was never the favorite friend of John F. Adlai suggested to Kennedy to offer carrots to the Soviets in return for the removal of weapons. He continues to say by urging Kennedy as Commander-in-Chief to abandon US naval bases at Guantanomo Bay and consider taking the Jupiters out of Turkey and Italy to realize a full demilitarization of Cuba. This was unpopular and McClone especially declared that it "pointed straight at our hearts" and that to give up now was completely wrong. Only a few days before, Sorensen had drafted a "quarantine speech" for total blockade meaning an "air strike means a US initiated Pearl Harbor on a small nation which history could neither understand nor forget." They were in discussion and approaching dangerous waters for an invasion with all its consequences which could be understood before it happened as militarily impractical". There were two different advantages to a blockade: 1) it was just more prudent and flexible to move for an air strike…without the Pearl Harbor posture.

2) it was the right step to block general war "while still causing the Soviets…to back down and abandon Cuba."

Though Kennedy had certain moments of doubt and changes of mind, he was always a cautious man who could ultimately make finer decisions above the rest. He met with former President Eisenhower who agreed in "blockade or full scale invasion of Cuba "with overwhelming force which seemed to him to be the only workable option. He had Eisenhower's full support either way. Kruschev by now believed they were "afraid" and had them running rings around him. This was misplaced understanding, for it could destroy forty cities and inflict millions of casualties on the American people. Kennedy was rattled enough by this point to send Anatol Dobrynin a letter for the attention of the Soviet Premier. This letter explicitly threatened nuclear war. The end of October between 24-30 "Operation Scaffardi" was dispatched. This was the beginning of the end of a long quarantine which was turned into an operation of prevention for blockade, passing out a full alert signal which was to stop and prevent the war from beginning at all. In London, Harold MacMillan wrote in his diary: "This is the first day of the world crisis." 90,000 marines and Air Force would hit the Cuban Island by October 30th. A dozen Polaris submarine with nuclear missiles on board were on their way to the Soviet seacoast. 60 BJ2s armed with hydrogen bombs were in their way carrying sealed envelopes with targets in mind.628 more bombers armed with nuclear weapons were dispersed to military and civilian airfields around the world. The American, Dean Acheson showed photographs to President Charles de Gaulle who said "tell President Kennedy that France will be with the US… it is exactly what I would have done. " By this it must be explained that Kennedy had outlined three points to his Office which were as follows:

1. Halt all offensive build-up; a strict quarantine on all offensive military equipment under shipment to Cuba.

2. …should these offensive military preparations continue, thus increasing the threat to this hemisphere, further action will be justified. I have directed the Armed Forces to prepare for any eventuality…

3. It shall be the policy of this Nation to regard any nuclear missiles launched from Cuba against any nation in the Western

Hemisphere as an attack by the Soviet Union on the US, requiring a full retaliatory strike upon the Soviet Union." He admitted privately. "the greatest danger of all would be to do nothing."

4. Later on in London, Prime Minister MacMillan wrote down in his diary after speaking to Kennedy. "This is the first day of the world crisis." When US Ambassador David K.E.Bruce in London came to show him the first U-2 photographs, MacMillan reacted quickly and revealed a lot by admitting: "Americans will realize what we in England have lived through for the past many years. The case was invading or trading" limiting military action into "quarantine". The entire nation was worried and literally scared of the impending doom on their country which some saw as a possibility. Students being the most frightened, with the alarming signals of impending war, broadcast everywhere in the news and media. For President Kennedy, it was a case of do or die. Indeed the greatest danger to the world would be "to do nothing." Though the US was prepared to react by now, the incident was accepted as a result of hostile action. Throughout the entire episode of quarantine, the Soviets remained obedient and true to the wishes of their situation regarding the US in Cuba. They too felt their peace threatened. They upheld their grace by showing a benign face offered by the President's ultimatum, who it can be said was showing a fist against Cuba, reinforced with strong sea and air defense. The media caught the attention of the world in a news headline of 26th October: "Everything to Prevent War" with another caption which read "reason must prevail." At any moment, the full attack by missiles positioned on stand-by was ready to be launched. This forced the Russians in their own territorial waters to back down and return home with their weapons on board. From this point of view, the quarantine was working well for the US. The Russians had, in a sense, cornered the US Government in a cold affront, sneaking weapons into Cuba for unknown reasons. For the American, it was to correct a course of catastrophe from hitting the US. The long trail with patience and time, helped develop the eventual theme of using "blockade" which forced through the inevitable conclusion that war would be necessary. At the worst, his political credibility was at stake, and the inevitable loss of Turkey and Italy and losses of the Jupiters there realized

for the Presidential entourage, the end of the beginning .In a phone call to Prime Minister MacMillan he told him: "If at the end of 48 hours, we are getting no place and the missile sites continue to be constructed, then we are going to be faced with some hard decisions. " The days that passed proved a stale mate between the Soviet Union and the US. The Soviets never stopped constructing their missiles, frustrating any agreement with their opponent. After letters with ultimatums were written in an exchange of letters or threats by both sides, by 30th October, Kruschev wrote: "Mr President, conditions are ripe for finalizing a treaty on cessation of nuclear weapons in three environments "-the atmosphere, outer space and under-water." By October, 1962, a settled agreement was made by which invasion by the US or any other country in the Western Hemisphere would not be involved. "The Soviet Government has sent to New York, USSR First Department Ministry of Finance, a Kuzenetsov with a view to assisting U Thant in his "noble effort" aimed at liquidation of the present dangerous situation. Then the President wrote to Kruschev vowing peace in the Caribbean with the same said in a letter to the Secretary General of the U.N.

5. In the two weeks following 27th October 1962, people would agree with Richard Reeves, author of "President Kennedy" who wrote: "many illusions were shattered in those two weeks, but a significant reality emerged too. At least two men, the two at the centre-Nikita Kruschev and John Kennedy-realized that no politician in his right mind was going to use nuclear weapons first. The price was too high, the judgement of history would be too severe. On Sunday afternoon, after the Soviet announcement for the maintenance of peace, they were aware that developments were approaching a point when events could become unmanageable."

6. It is very clear how the US were poised on the brink of a catastrophic war against Russia by contemplating an attack on the small island of Cuba. It is remarkable how a long pause and blockade preventing this course was set up by a relatively young President in the face of a Cuban missile crisis. He won majority poll ratings in the run up to the second term in office. His success has been well recorded in the letters and books

made of this period in time. We all know as well the eventual assassination of a most remarkable and brilliant man who we know as President Kennedy, his death bringing the world to mourn, never a President to be dismissed or forgotten from his troubled time of bargaining with the Soviets, and ending the episode in peace. The offer of a peace treaty accepted a full stop on nuclear bombs as offered by the Russian Premier, and was to be the touching stone for a pull back out of the evil strait it was headed for. These are the signs of the end of a beginning, for a greater and lasting condition to prevail as a world settlement. This was the revelation of John F Kennedy, who had worked for this to come about. Indeed, succees was his in his lifetime and together with Nikita Kruschev they fashioned the path for that eventual end.

CHAPTER 19

VIETNAM

While we have spoken of the way to find peace on our planet, we cannot avoid the fact of the Vietnam War. It is a little out of the way to exercise some sympathy for the Americans and the people of South Vietnam commencing around 1952, which I will start writing about. The war, as it has been publicized was a terrible one and probably one of the worst since World War 11, an era when life could "have been a dream" for many, but for a few, a nightmare of a hell never imagined before in history. When Kennedy entered Office, he wrote a letter to the Soviet leader which went as follows:

Dear Mr Chairman,

I agree with your thought that if we could find a measure of cooperation on some of these current issues, in itself, would be a significant contribution to the problem of igniting a peaceful and orderly world. I hope it will be possible, before too long, for us to meet personally for an informal exchange of views in regard to some of these matters…you may be sure, Mr Chairman, that I intend to do everything I can to forward developing a more harmonious relationship between out two countries." The letter dispatched into the hands of US information that the Russians were planning to put pressure on US British and French to force them out of the old West Berlin which stood by itself in an enclave controlled by the super-powers, East Germany was a territory occupied by the Soviets since the end of the War. The old German capital, Berlin, had been divided, after the War, into four sectors. These sectors were occupied by military units of the Soviet Union, the USA, GB, and France. There was a divided Berlin – East Berlin-West Berlin. This information produced a "Top Secret-Eyes Only" cable from Thompson to the White House. In the message, after a discourse with other diplomats and colleagues that "in the absence of negotiations, Kruschev will sign a separate peace treaty with East Germany and precipitate a Berlin Crisis this year" They expected East Germans to close off the sectors boundaries to control the flow of refugees-Kennedy himself thought that Berlin was the most dangerous place in the world. He believed that if a nuclear war should star, it might well begin there. The Americans thought as well that if Communists started up a military drive to control Europe, it would inevitably start in Berlin."

The Soviets always suspected the western interest was to reunify and rearm Germany to prevent the spread of Communism. It is true that a divided Berlin became the symbol and capitol of the Cold War effort. The interests for the American President was to change the way of the then present organization by setting up a task force which would not be able to get around "the man in the Oval Office". He was poised to take away much of their power and rights to maintain a situation which he considered of some importance and urgency. The "crisis of the day" was in Cuba, Laos, or Vietnam, the problems besetting his military as well as the deterrence used in gorilla warfare. Laos, for instance was unable to stand up and protect itself from being knocked down by Chinese Communists and their allies. Former President Eisenhower referred to Laos as "the cork in the bottle." It was a small kingdom with less than three million inhabitants.

Laos had been a French colony until 1954. The King was a King Savang Vatthana, head of the Royal Lao Government. His country had been in a civil war in a place called Lanxung, or "the land of many elephants". The King knew that his country was dependent on US aide and military defense as well which served to fight off the Pathet Lao (Patriotic Front) who in turn were backed up by Communists in North Vietnam. Each Laotian was given out $150 from a package of $300million. The king never wrote his own statements and speeches which were written by ghost-writers from the State Department. What they never wrote was the famous line: "My people only know how to sing and make love". When the President asked US Ambassador Winthrop Brown "what kind of people are these?" referring to Souvanna and Souphanouvong and Phoumi and King Kong Le. The frustrations mounted when Ambassador Winthrop Brown made himself very clear about this, who made the comment: "Laos is hopeless. It's just a series of lines on a map. Fewer than half the people speak Lao. They're charming, indolent, enchanting people, they're just not vigorous." He continued "the king is a total zero." He added "We were calling Kong

Le a Communist but he was actually a disgruntled soldier, a patriot rebelling against corrupt politicians. Souvanna Phouma, the political leader we were trying to get rid of, was the only leader with a remote chance of pulling the country together. "In another interview with Walt Lippman over lunch, he said: "As far as Laos is concerned, I don't see why we have to be more royalist than the King. India is more directly threatened than we are, and if they are not wildly excited, why should we be?" In the meanwhile, the Pathet Lao was taking one village after another and the President's choices were getting smaller as he realized that he either strayed and walked away for abandoning this country, allowing the Communists to take over, or deploying US troops as much as 10,000 to 60,000 personnel of the Joint Chiefs.

For this added expense, Okinawa saw the dispatch of 1400 combat Marines of the Fleet, and then 150 Marines to the Thai-Lao border. The NY Times read on March 21st: US READY TO FACE ALL RISKS TO BAR RED RULE OF LAOS. The fight was on against Communist domination. The region had been taken over by Communists and the real fight was the choice given to the President to decide which country he wanted to give aid to the most. It was a difficult choice for he did not want to let Laos down but on the other hand knew all along that for the Americans, the fight against Communism was of greater importance in Vietnam than in Laos. The stake involved realized the freedom and democracy to live free style in South East Asia for now and the future, or lose the whole to Communists and their way of fighting with cruelty in an unimaginable insurgency which was well publicized at the time. It was a war which he eventually put his mind to and decided to opt for which Lyndon Johnson, his successor would fight tooth and nail to win, even at moments when the sacrifices of American lives would cost more than he would have ever imagined.

Kennedy knew that Communists were attacking Laos. He knew as well Laos must keep up it's neutrality for the sake of the security of South East Asia. He knew as well that if this did not happen the region would be placed under a terrible threat to that security. To prove his earnestness and belief in freedom as a subjective understanding of that word in American terms, he made a promise on his Inauguration Day: "we shall pay any price, bear any burden, meet hardship, support any friend, oppose any foe, in order to assure the survival and success of liberty." During the Cold War, the US and Soviet Union played geopolitical games-Germany for instance was divided between East and West. Vietnam was divided between North and South as well as Korea. The North represented Communism in Vietnam and South Vietnam had a fight on, against the northern and communist neighbor. The Americans had taken on the substitute role of the French, after they left in order to fight for advancement of freedom and liberty against the insurgencies of the "Vietminh" as history must have warned earlier in the fiercest battles fought between the French and the North Vietnamese. The language spoken like a "mother tongue" was French rather than American style English. They had taken on a hard and difficult role, which would be the biggest test to overcome. The Vietnamese history proved a fierce race when in war and challenged by invasion and occupying forces. The importance of the French colony proved a turn of events that might have helped them find salvation in the midst of the terrible guerilla type conflict they were severely hit by. For instance, the US provided naval vessels, aircraft and arms to the French forces in Indochina and by 1952, was underwriting more than 40% of the cost of the war which ran into more than $800million. The French colonialism of Vietnam which lasted until 1952 was favored by the US Government. It was not to continue for in a battle at Diem Bien Phu, a large valley west of Hanoi, the North Vietnamese capitol, an attack occurred forcing the French who were in an "exposed position" to face a most surprising defeat. General Henri Navarre who was confident before the attack, felt assured that he and his forces could annihilate the Vietminh troops. The French had also Laos and Cambodia as colonies under their banner.

The overwhelming truth about addressing the Vietminh army whose creed was according to Mao Zedong "if the enemy advances, we retreat, if he halts, we harass. If he avoids battle, we attack. If he retreats, we follow. "Reluctance was felt by many on the US side and President Eisenhower said "it is simply beyond contemplation." He insisted that "there was just no sense in even talking of deploying US troops to replace French troops in Indochina. The Vietminh would simply turn their hate on the US to replace the one they felt against the French". To describe the French stand against the Communist Vietminh we must look at the intense fighting that took place in the first few days of 1954 when three divisions of Vietminh troops quickly ascended the hills surrounding the French garrison. A show of 50,000 Vietminh soldiers encircled the French. They were led by General Vo Nguyen Giap, who was no less than "the architect of a new strategic concept for guerilla warfare". His devastating belief was "accumulate a thousand small victories to turn into one great success!" Eisenhower kept up his stressed objections saying "I cannot tell you …how bitterly opposed I am to such a course of action…Indochina would absorb our troops for division!"…

By 7th May 1954, human wave attacks by Vietminh troops and fifty five days of bombardment with an estimated 1500 tons of ammunition, the French garrison was finally overwhelmed."

It was the sudden collapse of French colonialism which ended French supremacy of Laos, Cambodia and Vietnam which had been their colony up until May 1954, when an armistice ending French colonialism was signed. This automatically made independent states of those three countries. The newly appointed leader of Vietnam was NGO Dinh Diem, a Catholic Buddhist. The French puppet Emperor Bao Dai had been deposed. Diem knew only too well that his greatest opponent and enemy from the North was Ho Chi Minh and his followers.

President Kennedy was afraid he would lose the "cornerstone of the free world in South East Asia". He never believed that American military assistance in Indochina could "conquer an enemy which was everywhere but nowhere." At the same time, the map of that world had changed dramatically since the French surrender and withdrawal.

Soon after and by 1961, when Kennedy assumed power in Washington, South Vietnam was in full nationalist and communist upheaval losing its credibility and it's course. They were sinking into a mire of confusion. At the same time, a General Edward Lansdale, Deputy Secretary of Defense was sent to the region to write a report for the Government on how to cope with the new movement from the North. His report went along the lines that Vietnam's condition was a critical one and should be referred to a combat area of the Cold War "an area requiring emergency treatment". The US County Team Staff Committee, a Task Force in Saigon, stressed in their report that the South Vietnamese regime could be "toppled within a matter of months". What then would be Vietnam's fate? A conference meeting was formally held in Washington to try to answer this question. It was decided by 6th February that another deployment of American military would take place giving better assistance and bolster a collapsing regime that South Vietnam was enduring under their Diem. They would be under the direction of a General Leminitzer. The Presidential Task Force was to set off for Vietnam, and all prevention of Communist domination would be a program as continued by Robert McNamara. This plan would counter measure Communists from their plan to take over all South East Asia.27th April, the US commitment to re-enter Vietnam with more US combat troops was deployed and US marines, army and air force were dispatched. This is how the US entered the Vietnam War, a small step in what would be an initial step to assisting Saigon in a country which had been at War since 1952. This was to be the final mark of a war to stave off and fight off Communism which was almost considered like a "Satan" by Americans, who thought that Communists were evil and non-believers of the Christian faith. The Americans were prepared to fight a long and terrible war against the Vietcong! We can believe in the impropriety and intolerance and hate by wars created by Communist insurgents. By 3rd November, a further military Task Force was sent to operate US control. Robert McNamara never changed the American viewpoint when he said that America recommended committing themselves to the objective of preventing the fall of South Vietnam to Communism and the willingness to commit whatever US Combat Forces may be necessary to achieve this objective.

CHAPTER 20

KENNEDY'S VIETNAM CRISIS

5th August a Test Ban Treaty was officially signaled in Moscow. Present were the Secretary of State Dean Rusk and Adlai Stevenson, UN Ambassador. On the Russian side was Premier Kruschev who was present at this meeting. Dean Rusk would remind the Russian leader that the one country that had ever dropped bombs on other people, and did it twice, "and never think it may not happen again". Although Kennedy moved into these negotiations in Moscow, one remembers how the Vietnam War was to become a symbol of a Third World War for the US and American military fighting there. It is an irony, that while America was on a course of war to defend South Vietnam, deploying bombs at the same time the President was negotiating to toe in the Russians, signing a document recognized as an agreement to that effect.

The US Ambassador to Saigon was Henry Cabot Lodge. He was about to present his diplomatic credentials to the Government of Saigon. His main priority was to replace the leader of South Vietnam, Diem. His other worry was to meet up with press to discuss with them and complain about the photo shown world-wide of the monk Quang Duc, burning himself to death in protest. It was President Kennedy's insistence to uphold defense and it's arsenal as an emergency situation.

The pot was being stirred by the controlling new American side and military. Under order, both Diem and Nhu, started raiding pagodas in Saigon and Hue and more cities. They found those "communists in disguise" which brought forward arrests of 1400 monks, nuns and others from the monasteries. Another time, they raided with guns and shooting. "Chaos resulted in the surprise attacks and people came out to the streets beating on their gongs and drums waking up the city." They saw people dashing here and there and everywhere and charging on the Special Forces, who then used tear gas to drive the crowds back. Thirty were killed and many injured in Hue's "Dieu de Pagoda". Telephone and cable lines were cut off. This was what started the Buddhist agitation in Vietnam as well as in the US. Cabot Lodge was pessimistic about the leadership of Diem as well as Nhu. Vietnam held a history that had constantly endured tyranny, with a tyrant lasting not more than eight or nine years before his over-throw. Diem had already been in power for over nine years. It was to be agreed at a later meeting that Diem's time was up, and that a new leadership was to follow which was the main outlook discussed at the meeting in Hawaii.

The pagoda raids had been a deliberate and calculated risk before the arrival of Cabot Lodge. President Kennedy was expressly involved in organizing the moment for he wanted to avail the American side of control over the small state of South Vietnam. The Communists showed revulsions against Diem and Nhu. They, in turn wanted to push the Americans out. Diem was in poor political shape against the growing support and stance of the Buddhist monks. He may have outdone his own political usefulness. One remembers he was a Roman Catholic, seeking a vengeance against the Americans. Meanwhile, in America, anti-Buddhists campaigned against the War in Vietnam. The Vietnam Committee sent a petition signed by 1500 clergymen who clearly objected to military aid…"to those denied religious freedom…" It continued to protest against the spraying of chemicals for crops destruction as well as herding people into concentration camps called "strategic hamlets". This was flagrant violation of freedom and it's purpose to fight for it.

In an "Eyes Only" report sent by Cabot Lodge, he says only that another insurrection was about to take place as a direct result of an attempted plot for a coup. The army were to take the Presidential Palace. The two Vietnamese collaboration were Nguyn Dunh Thuan and General Tran Van Don. It was clear that Nhu had tricked the army into a proposed martial law by imposing the smashing dawn of pagodas with Police and Thuan's Special Forces loyal to him had put the eyes of the world and Vietnamese people into a state of martial law and military command. Cabot Lodge who we know wanted eventually to get rid of both Nhu and Diem, wrote how he could not find Nhu's actions in anyway tolerable. He felt Diem's chance was there to get rid of Nhu, and replace him with the best military and political person available at the moment. If Diem remains aloof and unsympathetic to these ideas. Cabot Lodge wrote, that he felt under those circumstances, that it was possible that Diem himself could not be "preserved". He forwarded his agreement as US Ambassador to help support and direct any "interim of breakdown" in the central government mechanism. Being as it was, the blame fell on Nhu and the order to achieve the objective as per say, went along the lines that a new leader must be found and elected. Finally, the American Ambassador and his team must find an alternative way to overthrowing the rule of Diem and find the ultimate replacement for him.

"We do not know how Washington will instruct us to achieve these objectives, but you will know that we give you our full support and backing, on action to achieve these objectives. It is necessary to minimize the essential information and take care of any potential leaks along the line." All this took place before the American Cabot Lodge had presented his credentials which he set out to do the following day at 11am.

In a reply cable from Washington, namely Ball, Harriman and Hilsman, the cable read that there was a crisis on in US whereby it was broadcast that last week's attack on the pagodas was not the responsibility of either Diem or Nhu in anti Buddhist action in Vietnam. They concluded that the pagoda raids had turned the people of Vietnam against Diem and Nhu.

The US Government agreed with the Ambassador that Nhu must go. They questioned the retention of Diem as leader. They could not make a decision or take action of assuming power of state. It was entirely up to them. If Nhu doesn't leave, and the Buddhist situation is not resolved, the State Department would find it impossible to keep military or economic support. They worried and hoped further bloodshed could be avoided and kept to a minimum risk situation.

While the cables flew back and forth, in Paris, France, French President Charles de Gaulle made a three paragraph statement. Both North and South Vietnam say that France would cooperate to rid their country of all "foreign influence". The Americans, if they liked, could ignore this declaration but on the other hand, if they did, it would heighten suspicions that Diem's brother Nhu would start talks with and accordingly settle his business with the North Vietnamese, an arrangement that would cancel the meaning of American presence. In a final, cable Lodge read: "I am reliably informed that the French

Ambassador Lalouette was with Nhu for four hours….also advised by a dependable source that he wants the US Government out of Vietnam so the French can become the intermediary between North and South Vietnam..I am reliably advised that Nhu is in a highly volatile frame of mind and that some sort of gesture through Nhu to North Viet Nam is not impossible."

CHAPTER 21

THE END OF A CRISIS

Immediately after Kennedy's death, Lyndon Johnson, his Vice President, was sworn in as the new.

News about Vietnam was not favorable, and there was talk of neutralizing South Vietnam. French President Charles de Gaulle told US Ambassador Bohlen that he though the US mission was "doomed and that negotiations constituted the only realistic course." He believed that the United States had become embroiled in a conflict in Vietnam that was essential that was essentially the same as the French had encountered at the end of World War II. De Gaulle believed in the neutralization of South Vietnam and that a Geneva conference that included China was the "best course available to the United States." Johnson listened to his Joint Chiefs of Staff, who preferred to continue the warfare against North Vietnam. They wanted air raids to attack both military and industrial targets in North Vietnam, the mining of harbors, "imposition of a naval blockade, and in the event China intervened, the possible use of nuclear weapons." The President told McGeorge Bundy on the phone to "get in or get out." Of course, Congress had to approve any official course of action. South Vietnam was losing its battle for freedom and independence and could have easily fallen into communist control, but the Americans doubted that reports coming in from Saigon were valid. A serious communication breakdown between

Ambassador Lodge and General Harkins had occurred, bringing about manipulations via propaganda by Diem's provincial officers, which had been going on for some time. McNamara complained about the committee of a dozen generals who were "playing the government role and missing out on their real duties." McNamara trusted one army leader, Major General "Big" Minh, the chairman of the executive committee of the Revolutionary Council and president of the provisional government. Although McNamara had strongly recommended that Minh take full control of the country himself, McNamara doubted that there was "the necessary will to power there." Bundy let President Johnson know that that Vietnam was critical to winning or losing the 1964 presidential election that was coming up. Although the Kennedys had hoped to keep their name beside the Johnson administration at the White House, there was too much opposition to appointing Robert Kennedy as Johnson's running mate, as Johnson himself simply did not like him. When the time came to consider a candidate, Johnson chose Hubert Humphrey of Minnesota as his running mate, a sore disappointment for Bobby and the Kennedy family.

CHAPTER 22

DALLAS TEXAS

The Presidential car and security were campaigning for a new term of office. Sitting in his convertible car with his wife Jackie next to him, we know, a marksman in a building over-looking the boulevard that the motorcade of cars and security passed, the President was suddenly shot many times by a riffle aimed at him from that building. The assassin had ties with Russia and they believe he worked for the Russians. We need to remember that by the time he died, a total of 108 US military personnel had been killed in Vietnam. The final total would be more than 58,000 a few years later after the assassination of President Kennedy.

In the movie made years ago, the approval of the CIA in the killing of the President of the USA was the momentum of the filming " Death of a President". In the court room drama, it was surmised the President was both a Roman Catholic, spoke with a Boston accent rather than a Harvard accent, and sympathized with the blacks, and worked for civil rights, who in the eyes of the CIA are never accepted in high government. The pawn in the conspiracy must have been the assassin himself. He speaks with eloquence and with the intelligence gathering he does himself sensitively driving the case to a climax concluding that it must have been a plot executed by the CIA who were everywhere that day, watching the motorcade as much as the assassin named and convicted for the crime and coup. In this movie, the CIA are the ones cited as the villains. This much is true. The reason may not be so obvious to anyone, but in terms of modern day language, they could have said it was the "Rouble" that paid up. This mystifies many who may not have ever come to terms with their "Financial Sven" then called "Jack Rouble."

Typically, the world mourned the loss of the American President, and he was buried at Arlington Cemetery, a never to be forgotten great and young President whose assassination stopped his work for humanity and for the causes most celebrated by Americans being love of freedom and democracy.

The plot aggravated by Cabot Lodge's immediate reaction to both Diem and Nhu staggers the writer for the way his control and hand to carry out his plot went through under the secret veil of a diplomatic front. The man who wielded such power went beyond his own expectations. Historians may wish to comment on the betrayal set out from the meeting in Hawaii when that fatal day in 1965, the South Vietnam ruler and his brothers were finally, as Cabot Lodge would have said in his own words "got rid of." Never could it have been done for personal gain nor could it have been done for any other reason than as stated before, being South Vietnam needed a new ruler. This apparently was Cabot Lodge's idea which materialized regardless.

In July 1954, France signed an armistice, ending French colonialism in South East Asia, thereby creating the separate states of Vietnam, Laos and Cambodia. Vietnam was divided between the North and the South, the North infiltrated by the Vietminh "alliance" and the South by "western powers". This agreement "called for nationwide elections in 1956" which banned any presence of foreign troops and foreign military bases. The newly appointed leader of Vietnam was NGO Dinh Diem, a Catholic over mainly Buddhists. Diem when he came to power won ninety nine percent of the votes having deposed along the way, the French puppet Emperor Bao Dai. He knew realistically speaking that he did not hold all the power in contest against the likes of his opponent from the North, Ho Chi Minh and his followers.

Concerning the fate of Vietnam, Kennedy introduced General Lemnitzer on 6th of February to ensure that the South Vietnamese army was deployed more coherently. "I would think that the re-distribution of available forces immediately would make them more effective."

MacGeorge Bundy recalls the President's growing interest in assisting Saigon "at levels of conflict short of the engagement of U.S. combat troops."

He remembered "advice and support, especially on unconventional warfare, were attractive" and he remained "regularly on the side of a diversified and innovative effort "that would enhance South Vietnam's ability to confirm "the growing insurgency".

An increase in expenditure and manpower were employed." Bundy also recalls that "both of these expansions were large against what he had before, and small compared for what came later.

By April, Kennedy had appointed Deputy Secretary of Defense Roswell & Gilpatrick to head the Presidential Task Force in Vietnam. Robert McNamara had sworn that he would confirm and have a program to prevent Communist damnation of South Vietnam. "It ties down any proposal of a Communist master plan to take over all of South East Asia. By now, 27th April, a report moved on to say the U.S. was committed to sending a small contingent of U.S. combat troops as a symbol of American commitment to South Vietnam. U.S. Marines, army and air force were dispatched to support and assist South Vietnamese combat forces. This is how the U.S. entered the Vietnam War, showing a smaller step in what transpired after this initial step to assist Saigon in a country which had been at war, never regaining peace since 1952. It had to be done as a commitment by the US, to prevent Communist insurrection which might have broken the agreement of dividing North and South. The President may have done what was politically considered correct to do, on the understanding that America could not allow further infiltration of Communism to take over South East Asia. This was the immediate problem. Many have voiced their opinion about American involvement in Vietnam, and even though they struggled long and hard over this issue, Americans fought a hard and terrible war which has been talked of often enough. In "Lessons in Disaster" we can read about the impropriety of intolerance and hate of wars created by Communists. By November 3rd, a proposal was made to the President to send in a further military Task Force to operate under U.S. control."

By 5th November, it was agreed that a deployment of eight thousand men should be considered "only part of a potentially larger commitment of combat troops. They were thinking in fact of sending a "vast American ground force commitment to defend South Vietnam from its communist insurgency. McNamara it is said was by now recommending the Americanization of the Vietnam War". The reasoning never changed as they continued to recommend "to commit ourselves to the objective of preventing the fall of South Vietnam to Communism and the willingness to commit whatever U.S. Combat Forces may be needed to achieve this objective."

CHAPTER 23

PRESIDENT JOHNSON'S PREOCCUPATION WITH VIETNAM

After President Kennedy's assassination, the Vice President Lyndon B Johnson took over the Presidency and the White House.

His policy regarding Vietnam took on a more serious note and he declared: "that Americans were not doing enough for South Vietnam". In fact he delivered the self-imposed restriction as it was set by his predecessor, by admitting aerial bombings of critical targets in North Vietnam and reinforced more US military to target and take more direct action against North Vietnam. This would eventually lead the way for America to have the "Americanization of the Vietnam War."

South Vietnam was pursued by rebellion and though a new Government had been established by a younger military regime, their General Nguyen Kanh was soon over-thrown.

The growing developments in Vietnam forced Charles de Gaulle, President of France to reiterate his belief that the choice was to accept possible collapse of our counter-insurgency efforts or the escalation of the conflict toward a direct military confrontation of North Vietnam by the USA. By November, there was talk of neutralizing South Vietnam but in Paris, President Charles de Gaulle felt the deployment in it's entirety was doomed to failure and that the only way forward was through negotiation. Although America had unreserved rights in the War, which they felt would be won by their rejecting claims that it could not be won, de Gaulle's attitude was that the position was too rigid amongst the military state. He also felt that a negative position was in hand "by bolting the doors in South East Asia" with no further purpose to "fall back on". The Democratic leaders thought that if they did not pay attention to the French proposal, Vietnam could end up bringing their own worst disaster ending in a "humiliating defeat or withdrawal" and costing more than the previous Korean War.

By March 1964, Johnson was advised by de Gaulle who saw no particular future in talks with the Americans, to seek the Geneva Conference Meeting to demand the neutralization of Vietnam for he felt this was the only option left open to them. He realized the American Government had become "embroiled" in a conflict which the French had encounterd at the end of World War 11.

There were four commitments the US fought for. They were as follows:

1) Americans against terror and fanatics

2) Americans keep their commitment

3) America wants to keep peace as their objective

4) Bundy was to go to Congress to get approval for further and stronger military operations against North Vietnam.

With ongoing attacks against the North Vietnamese fanatics, McGeorge Bundy recommended to the President to increase the bombing, realizing it would be impossible to take them completely because of their ability to seek shelter by retreating into the jungle. From this point of view, America might have known from the beginning that jungle warfare would eventually force withdrawal from both sides with an eventual stale-mate as the situation in the progress report in the conflicts.

It has been said often and reported as well as written, that President Johnson though of the same political Democratic Party, disliked his predecessor's younger brother, Robert Kennedy, a man who worked for civil rights and did much for the Black Community. President Johnson's stance toward Vietnam became an ideologue. He wished to over-throw the Vietcong and it's army and ordered large scale bombing and the deployment of ground troops. Although this added greater measures and stiffer aggression by the fanatical North Vietnamese, General Westmoreland realized that they must allow and accept a larger scale American sacrifice. He claimed that he believed the faith of America rested on the years starting from 1961 with a war against the Vietcong and the enormity of the Communist problem which gave rise to American assertion which must realize greater military presence there then before. They would fight the North Vietnamese Forces until the bitter end! In essence what he thought at the time was most unlike the option held by Thompson. The newly appointed Ambassador Taylor doubted whether ground troops could successfully combat and defeat the insurgency. He deliberated called history a successful anti-guerilla campaign with a 10-1 chance to develop superiority over the guerillas. He objected in principle to ground troops and asked for a recall for air strikes trying to establish this as a more affirmative step in the right direction. Obviously, he and the President were at odds with each other, and though the Ambassador was a dignitary amongst American Generals, he and the President were not in agreement about this.

He claimed that he believed the faith of America rested on the years starting from 1961 concerning a war against the Vietcong and the enormity of the Communist problem which gave rise to American assertion which must realize a greater military presence there then before to fight the North Vietnamese Forces till their end!

The Americans had hoped to deteriorate the forces of the side that was in fact winning the war. Although American presence influenced stability in the region, most of the fighting which was subversive terrorism was being operated by the South Vietnamese. It was to become a painful process of declining warfare for the South Vietnamese. During a visit requested by Ambassador Taylor, one of the Presidents over Bundy, who toured Vietnam was overwhelmed by the news during this time of American casualties suffered by his soldiers in a territory bordering and connecting to South Vietnam's "central highlands." It was adjacent to Cambodia and Laos. The strikes carried out against South Vietnam army headquarters usually protected by US troops killed nine Americans, wounded one hundred thirty seven and forced evacuation of seventy-six. This, Bundy felt was a deliberate "provocation" to coincide with his tour, and mission for South Vietnam. However, the North Vietnamese leader, Dang Vu Hiep, denied this, referring to the incident which had been planned weeks in advance and with no knowledge of Bundy's presence in that country.

"The situation in Vietnam is deteriorating" warned Bundy. They discussed "game theory" part of a study for "international security affairs." There was to be a bombing campaign-"perpetual" in its attacks and consistency of "gradual and sustained reprisal."

Eventually it was Bundy who realized that the war may be won by the North Vietnamese whose "skill in their sneak attacks and ferocity when cornered" were extraordinary in spite of their own losses they always returned for more!

The point he had to make writes Gordon Goldstein, is "At a minimum it will damp down the change that we did not do all that we could have done, and this change will be important in many countries, including our own. The odds of success with accuracy may be somewhere between 25% and 75%" he said. He continued and acknowledged "what we can say is that even if it fails, the policy will be worth it."

So the idea of the "bombing strategy" was discussed and eventually agreed upon for it avoided the ground forces attacks. "While the proposal to use tactical nuclear weapons against North Vietnam, never gained "traction" Bundy…believed Eisenhower's influence on Johnson was significant. Eisenhower's advice at the time "you must fight to win. Dean Rusk (Secretary of State) said the US must remain "reliable" and is "a friend who means what he says." Eisenhower agreed with Westmoreland that South East Asia "must not fall under communist beginnings."

However, the French Foreign Minister, Maurice Couve de Murville, said at the time that he did not "honestly think they could "avoid defeat in South Vietnam". The Americans comforted themselves that the Frenchman had "obvious reasons" for saying this. In his Cabinet, the President was given similar warnings agreeing with the French. One amongst them was Hubert Humphrey who declared that the risks of American involvement in Saigon was near-equal to a Third World War which had been avoided during the Korean War. Humphrey asked the President to accede to the demand to stop American intervention before it was too late that the president was "in a stronger position to do this than any administration in this century." Johnson was so annoyed that he banned Humphrey from further participation in the War Game!

President Johnson had all but committed America to the

Americanization of the Vietnam War. The point was further struck home when Taylor advised the Presidency that ground defense with it's forces was a way of combat against guerilla Vietcong forces. He admitted the French had done the same years before and that they had been badly defeated as he thought the US would face the same fate. Taylor said in a word "when I view this array of difficulties I am convinced that we should adhere to our past policy of keeping ground forces out of direct counter insurgency role…"Taylor's advice was rejected and on 26th February, the Secretary of State, Dean Rusk, informed the US Embassy in Saigon, of an "imminent deployment of new US forces – "3,500 marines, were sent and landed in South Vietnam by 8th March 1965, with ground combat units deployed in mainland Asia, not done since the Korean war. Thus the Americanization of the Vietnam War had commenced. It is true to state that General Johnson at this point warned the President that "it would take 500,000 troops five years to win the war." In the meanwhile, Bundy advised the President to dismiss the US Ambassador in South Vietnam. This was to do with diplomats only, regarding representatives of a country whose military intervention kept "American opinion from division and criticism". Thanks to diplomacy the American deployment was seeking, a way of finding an "eventual settlement" in Vietnam. The main objective in the political strata reveals how the cost of the war was relative to the protectionism of their own global credibility which was not to render the U.S. being looked on as a "paper tiger." Military defeat was acceptable of the high cost of the war, even deploying more than 100,000 troops which stamped the accomplished fact of the Americanization of the war. It is agreed that the obvious policy held by Kennedy was "reversed without a doubt". His "no combat-troop policy" was not contained in the Johnson take-over after his death. By now, US forces were committed to a great fight on the Vietnamese territory participating in offensive guerilla warfare, which they were unequal to match.

At one point, the Americans went to talk with Soviet Communist Russia about enforcing a peaceful settlement in Vietnam. They offered "economic carrots" to Hanoi, but Hanoi's control, direction and encouragement for Vietcong presence was written about but no further progress was made by the Russians to settle the disputed matter concerning the territories. The war then escalated and turned the progress into an offensive which forced the Presidency firstly of deploying 100% more troops when the previous year 150% more troops had been sent in only to acknowledge belief that it was all a stale mate and nothing had been achieved either side. The US determination did not prevail and the fighting continued in spite of "very demoralized forces." The Americans refused to quit. The Americans could not find their own leadership even by counter measures to stop the intolerable war and their own forces struggling through jungle lands to fight excessive and difficult terrain for guerilla warfare. Their offer to settle their dispute peacefully was rejected. It was a case of a "no way" for this leadership as far as Hanoi was concerned.

Hanoi was never to satisfy Saigon and "vice versa". Saigon, in this war game, was compelled to follow a path that could only lead to their "early collapse." The conclusion was determined by now and though the bombing strikes on North Vietnam continued, it could lead to no purpose as no negotiation was possible. Later on, President Charles de Gaulle offered his advice to the Johnson people to try settling for a peace treaty in a Geneva Conference. This was accepted. It was agreed at the Geneva Conference that the bombing had solidified North Vietnam's determination to continue advanced guerilla war efforts. The Foreign minister, Nguyen Khac Nuynh said "The bombing was the key factor." The ceasefire of the bombing was also the "key factor." The US bombing was a challenge to the sovereignty of North Vietnam he said.

Tran Quang Co who was first deputy foreign minister said that bombings were a critical part to national morale in North Vietnam. "Never before", he said "did the people of Vietnam from top to bottom , unite as they did during the years of US bombings.

Ho Chi Minh's appeal was that "nothing is more precious than freedom and independence" and this statement certainly went straight to the "hearts and minds of the Vietnamese people."

The War Games of the American National Security and their advisers demonstrated and afterwards was discussed by the Communists of North Vietnam as a "massive determination and endurance of Vietnamese Communist forces which should never have been in doubt."

The old saying by Bundy returned to haunt the White House, "that it was better to fight and lose in Vietnam than not fight at all". After the event and as an afterthought, it is said that Bundy admitted "If Lyndon Johnson in 1965 had viewed Vietnam in the way John Kennedy had in 1961, Bundy would have subordinated his own convictions to the President's very different determination that the war in Vietnam should not become an American enterprise." Bundy had argued the point about the pros and cons of going into the war and said "Straight out-it's a loser-so lose it as cheaply as you can." In the meanwhile, President Johnson's administration set up ground combat forces to launch "unconstrained volley of endurance tests, encounter casualties and numbers." Bundy wrote in his memos... that it was "a major error and we failed even to address it. At the end or war or peace, Bundy recollected how different Kennedy was to Johnson, having known both of them well. "Of Kennedy, he said this of him: "I think he would not have expanded the war. He would have found a way to negotiate it. He would not have a US ground war." He wrote again a few weeks before he died. "Kennedy does not have to fear any man as a greater authority."

CHAPTER 24

REMEMBRANCE OF PRESIDENT KENNEDY

The years after President Kennedy's death, Vietnam was to be known as America's largest war when the country would be defeated for the first time. While he was alive, he had two messages to give concerning Vietnam. It is said that his two proposals could not have existed together. His first view was that" we must not quit there."

His second message was that at the end it was up to the Vietnamese to do their job by themselves meaning without the help of American intervention. One cannot know what he would have done at the end.

Bundy arrived at the conclusion in the final years when he reviewed the history of this war, and discussed this with his colleagues, that Kennedy would never have deployed ground combat forces nor would he have Americanized the war. He thought Kennedy would never have wanted it to be a "big item" on his agenda. It was not a balance of power or anything other than an American political opinion. The "opportunity" was lost when Kennedy fell and was replaced by Johnson. He believes that had Kennedy lived, there would have been no Vietnam War. Johnson came to power in the White House, the war took on the tune of the tragedy that would unfold in history books and media coverage as it was not destined to be under Kennedy.

Bundy had served both Presidents Kennedy and Johnson, and each undertook to make decisions or not make them, which carried with it the final responsibility of a final authority as Commander-in-Chief. One knows no US combat troops could be dispatched without the final approval of the Commander-in Chief. The ultimate responsibility was "his" and his alone, which both Presidents understood all too well. As Bundy, we know, respected and liked both Presidents, each became a larger than life character and "more tragic" for the former.

Bundy declared that Kennedy's "no combat troop policy" was of the greatest significance for American historians writing or reading about this hellish war. Lyndon Johnson, it is undisputed, made a decision reversing Kennedy's policy and America found itself thick into the heavy artillery in a war which could not have happened, had Kennedy survived.

McGeorge Bundy never himself felt confident about the war which he knew could not be won. On the other hand, his priority was to try to force the North to withdraw and see the fall of Communism in that region of the world. This is what he couldn't let go of as the top priority to help the President lead the way into the Vietnam War. He did not believe South Vietnam could "overhaul" Communism or its insurgencies. He knew the way was tough and the course almost impossible. On both sides, they embarked on a "hopeless war." They had practically no chance of it being won by the allied forces of America and South Vietnam. Chinese Communists were stronger than a monster. The human cost of the war was never under scored and though the hope of seeing an end of the war with the Americanized forces negotiating for a settlement with Hanoi controlling a united Vietnam, Kennedy's policy of 1961 might have been a policy drafted in 1965! There was no "happy ending" to this near World War 111 , and what transpired and already discussed were the events of 1965 when the war stopped. One note of criticism is that both Presidents never publicly made known their policies concerning Vietnam. Though Kennedy now was considered right and Johnson possibly too committed to a war that could not be won, one remembers that after his death, they wanted to work on a post coup process. It has been a theory that President Kennedy had been killed by a CIA conspiracy because of his belief in civil rights. Apart from these two demoting factors about him, he was considered even worse by the CIA on the grounds of his Roman Catholic beliefs. This would bring the history book on a possible new promotion of a link with United States Intelligence Services who it can be said, may have participated in his early death but as stated before, this is truly doubtful. A theory conceived in a movie which took me by surprise as an eventual "update" in a Hollywood style drama of a secrecy which could never be exposed as anything other than a Hollywood drama must have been the original "Conspiracy Theory" Part 1.

The elderly and former General MacArthur said, after a talk with Robert Kennedy, "that we would be foolish to fight on the Asiatic continent and that the future of South East Asia should be determined at the diplomatic table." He continued saying to Kenneth O'Donnell" there was no end to Asia and even if we poured a million American infantry soldiers into that continent, we would still find ourselves outnumbered on every side." This made an important impression on President Kennedy and influenced his thinking with respect to South East Asia. "His whole attitude was changed and he took the side of General MacArthur that went to undermine the thoughts and advise of his Joint Chiefs of Staff… "Well, now, you gentlemen, you go back and convince General MacArthur than I'll be convinced."

It is interesting to note that at a lunch meeting with a NY Times Columnist, in October 1961, at the moment when he was pressured about deployment of ground combat troops to Vietnam Krock, the columnist wrote in his diary; " The President still believes in what he told the Senate several years ago, that US troops should not be involved on the Asian mainland, especially in a country with the difficult terrain of Laos and inhabited by people who don't care how the East West dispute as to freedom and to resolve self determination. Moreover, said the President, the US can't interfere in civil disturbances created by guerillas, and it was hard to prove that this wasn't largely the situation in Vietnam."

At the same time, Kennedy received a memorandum from JK Galbraith, then US Ambassador to India, sent in April 1962. In this brief message, Galbraith warned Kennedy of "growing military commitment" which could "expand step by step into a major, long-drawn out indecisive military involvement." His advice was to "resist all step which commit American troops to combat action and impress upon all concerned the importance of keeping American forces out of actual combat commitment."

Kennedy summarizing the point of the war was to hit the North hard but recognized the importance of the Ho CHI MINH TRAIL as the path that helped resupply the Vietcong in the South "No matter what goes wrong… or whose fault it really is, the argument will be that Communists have stepped up their infiltration and we can't win unless we hit the north. These trails are a built-in excuse for failure, and a built-in argument for escalation." The re-elections were looming over the White House and Kennedy's determination to win the second term, forced his attention once more on Vietnam. He told Mike Mansfield that he wanted an eventual but complete withdrawal from Vietnam and would according to a press conference later on, in May 1963 "withdraw all the troops, any numbers of troops, any time the Government of South Vietnam would suggest it."

He hardly wanted to be called "a Communist appeaser." He realized his re-election was the main priority on his agenda. He must win the American stand in South Vietnam. This was a case where action must be taken by South Vietnam to oust them from their position – "put a government in there that will ask us to leave". This was his "easy" answer when asked privately how he might "engineer an American withdrawal."

CHAPTER 25

PRESIDENT RONALD REAGAN

REYKJAVIK 12ᵀᴴ OCTOBER,1986

Gorbachev and Reagan were to meet for talks on nuclear disarmament. Gorbachev invited Reagan to a meeting in Reykjavik and handed him a list of consolidation to drop nuclear defense as listed here.

1. strategic arms

2. medium range missiles

3. The treaty or limitation of Anti-Ballistic missiles (ABM) systems. An agreement was made to prevent any withdrawal from this Treaty for the next ten years, abiding by these agreements throughout this period of time. Tests carrying out "space based elements of anti-ballistic missile defenses in space will be prohibited".

The American people were "astonished and excited" by this offer of peaceful determination to decommission.

The ABM Treaty was good for Americans-but expansion on it was their preference.

Reagan wanted "to turn the clock back to the 1920's" when there were no ballistic missiles or nuclear bombs. He says in his own words "wouldn't it be great if we could make the world as safe today as it was then?" This was his dream and his imagination working for deployment which the meeting succeeded in establishing between the two parties.

The U.S, included in the negotiations a better progress so that "we do not need ten years" as he relied on it taking a shorter time for this progress to be made.

Gorbachev asked for a share in "oil-well equipment, digitally guided machine tools, or even milking machines. News "blacked out" negotiations. Gorbachev wanted "perestroika". Reagan whose talks with the Soviet leader succeeded in mutual agreement of arms talks.

By eliminating Soviet or American missiles in Europe, this was to be "zero option" as referred to by Reagan.

With respect to SDI the President recalled that he had made a pledge to the American people that SDI would contribute to disarmament and peace and not be an offensive weapon…it would be a threat to no one…"This was the way the ABM Treaty of Reykjavik Iceland was formed.

The point affirmed by both leaders was that potential nuclear threat must be eliminated. Joint efforts to prevent a nuclear madman from taking over the enlightened peace agreement which in turn would provide protection, but it would be a "limited protection", it was almost a case of dancing to the tune along the lines that "it takes two to tango" meaning the Gorbachev's application to the President to position himself to the Soviet position as it was then.

The Soviet's asked for more understanding over the Soviet proposals as it came. They were:

1) 50% cuts in heavy weapons

2) The INF cuts

3) Restrictions to test all connected to the ABM moves.

At the end of their talk, the Americans wrote down the offer in a 100 worded document which was as follows:

1. Both sides would agree to confine themselves to reserve, development and testing which is permitted by the ABM Treaty, for a period of 5 years, through 1991, during which time a 50% reduction of strategic nuclear arsenals would be achieved. This being done, both sides will continue the pact of reductions

with respect to all remaining ballistic missiles with the goal of all ballistic missiles by the end of the 10 year period, with all offensive ballistic missiles eliminated, either side would be free to introduce defenses.

2. Although not fully "clinched" as a perfect deal, opposed by some of the President's closest advisors, it was agreed in principle in so far as the ABM Treaty went.

3. SDI was America's guarantee that if the Soviets went back on their commitment to defense, their nuclear program may give over their agreement solidified by the ABM Treaty of 1991, in Reykjavik, Iceland. They parted in good company, in accord with each other agreeing to a decision that would "lead to a safer world without nuclear weapons.

When Gorbachev returned to the Kremlin, he told his 16 Politburo "I did all I could, but only a madman could go ahead with arms control, while the U.S is developing a space weapons system. " His anger and frustration declared itself as he described it: "When Reagan bid me farewell, he could not bring himself to look in my eyes." He continued claiming:" After Reykjavik, we collected more scores in our favor there after Geneva. In a way we traded sides with the Americans. Before we usually lagged behind them in promoting our information for consumption in the outer world. We were late to giving views, conducting press conferences. This process should be developed further. Reykjavik must become a new beginning for our propaganda. It should acquire a more aggressive character."

Reagan on the other hand confused many though he carefully spelled out the meaning behind the ABM and the SDI.

The headlines of the Press reports such as the NY Times was full of leaks and mis-information, as the Officials in both Washington and Moscow tried to re-write the history of those days in Iceland when the two Poles met.

Basically, the October 29th 199 6 headlines read, for example "U.S says two leaders spoke of giving up all nuclear arms."

On October 26th as well, read "Reagan is quoted by Soviet on end of all Atom arms "etc.

However in Britain, the Prime Minister, then Margaret Thatcher was put off the agreement which opposed Great Britain's agreement to nuclear defense, and it's modernization. "Her whole political future was at stake." The opposition Labour Party however were at that time in agreement with President Reagan's idea to eliminate nuclear weapons on British soil. They stood with Reagan at the time against Prime Minister Thatcher.

At home, Henry Kissinger spoke in a news show: "Where one side suddenly spring a major plan, on the other, one expects it to be negotiated in 36 hours, that's the preposterous and outrageous." On the other hand, Secretary of Defense, James Schleshinger thought that in principle it defied national security and it's establishment. He wrote: "For a generation, the security of the World War has rested on nuclear attack but also massive conventional assault from the East... The American position at Reykjavik seemed to have reflected no understanding of this simple fundamental..."The SDI did more to protect the US than get rid of the country's nuclear arsenal.

Of Perestroika, we have learned of Gorbachev's plan for "a new world" where "the use or threat of force no longer can be an instrument of foreign policy." This was to be the age of perestroika which pledged liberalizing immigration laws and human rights practices in the Soviet Union. The delegates and Officials all around the world were taken aback and completely baffled by his entre into the solar system with his ideals and intentions to revolutionize the plan for Perestroika. I will now explain its meaning which he addressed at the U.N. Headquarters in New York City on December 6th.

"Today I can report to you that the Soviet Union has taken a decision to reduce its armed forces. Within the next two years their numerical strength will be reduced by 500,000 men. The number of conventional armaments will also be substantially reduced. This will be done unilaterally...By agreement with our Warsaw Treaty allies, we have decided to withdraw 1991 six tank divisions from the German Democratic Republic, Czechoslovakia and Hungary, and to disband them...Soviet forces in these countries will be reduced by 50,000 men and their armaments, by 5000 tanks...At the same time, we shall reduce the numerical strength of the armed forces in this part of our country and the territories of our European allies will be reduced by 10,000 tanks, 8500 artillery systems and 800 combat aircraft."

The Soviet Union were pulling out of a game which had threatened the western hemisphere and reduced the Red Army's tanks which had been present in Europe for more than forty years! He moved the Soviet troops out of Asia "beginning in the Mongolian People's Republic." The brilliant play was considered a non plus for him and the Soviet Union and as far as the New York Daily News was concerned, they referred to him as the "Soviet sorcerer." Newsweek said that he was "playing a losing hand." However the New York Times applauded him saying "Perhaps not since Woodrow Wilson presented his Fourteen Points in 1918 or since Franklin Rooselevelt and Winston Churchill promulgated the Atlantic Charter in 1941 has a world figure demonstrated the vision Michail Gorbachev displayed at the United Nations." The New York Post apparently thought this "It is one thing to negotiate with him, another to give aid and still another to celebrate him. They curtly said "the first proposition is acceptable. The latter two are not." It became the talk of New York and the world over.

Later on, commiserating over their past talks Reagan handed the Soviet leader a framed photograph of their first meeting in Geneva in a boathouse. The inscription on it read: "We have walked a long way together to clear a path for peace. ...Gorbachev asked Reagan at this point what he thought of his U.N. speech. Reagan admitted "I heartily approve." After all, it was not often a Soviet leader pushed for democracy in front of the whole world and he must have wondered if he was making himself at all popular with anyone. He was in the middle "of a delicate transition" with Reagan and Bush attending and as witnesses of the fact.

After the Reykjavík summit meeting, Gorbachev said to some students in Moscow "of democracy is a system of government than it is a system to keep government limited…"The American President who came to visit a few months later was asked to explain what the meaning of the Constitution was. Reagan's reply was: "Our Constitution is different"-it is better explained in these three words "we the people…" Our Constitution is a document in which we the people tell the Government what it's powers are "It's hard for Government planners no matter how sophisticated, to even substitute for millions of individuals working day and night to make this dream come true…"

The Americans looked critically at their President with his arms on Gorbachev's schedule walking around in Red Square in Moscow committing to their belief that Russia was the "Evil Empire" of cold hearted Communists."

After his visit and his return to the U.S he said:" We know the power of the word and we know the importance of being able to speak directly to the Soviet people without their Government in between. I was pleased on my trip to convey the support of the American people directly to the dissidents and refuseniks struggling for their human rights and also to the clergy with regard to freedom of religion."

Of style, and of characteristics of the man, he was devoted to the one, being his wife Nancy. Otherwise he was a "warmly ruthless man" and if you were in his way, he got rid of you, after all his decision was a matter for the Oval Office. He didn't like hurting people however.

CHAPTER 26

CRISIS OF KOREAN AIRLINE

The plane was shot down by missile by Russians over Russian airspace. Reagan's attitude, as actor "vengeance isn't the name of the game." Over-reaction was "Korean airline massacre for after all, Francois Mitterand of France believed that "the world was as close to war as it had been during the Cuban Missile crisis in 1962. Pope John Paul 11 was in agreement.

Of Reagan it is written that he was a person "more interested in theatrical truth than in empirical truth."

Reagan was not, so it is written, "a man of vision, he was a man of imagination – and he believed in the past he imagined."

CHAPTER 27

30 MARCH 1981
ASSASINATION ATEMPT
CRISIS.

John W Hinkley a young student at Yale University was a loner, who had seen the movie "Taxi Driver" with Jodie Foster, and had fallen in love with her. His gun that pulled on President Reagan, while Reagan was on his way back from the AFL-CIO's Building Construction Trades Department at the Hilton Hotel in Washington DC, where he gave a speech to a national conference. A pressman called out "Mr President..." when the sound of "pop pop pop" was heard, and the immediate surprise stunned the President who did not realize he had been shot as he asked Jerry Parr his Secret Service agent "What the hell's that?" Parr was "tackling" the President and pushing him into the limousine floor, which had bullet proof windows. He ordered the driver to "take off" and shouted to him to "get the President to the White House." The secret service agent who went on a "jump seat" and attended to the President feeling his side and back for blood or injury. Reagan sat "stiff" on the seat and coughed up blood. "I think I've cut my mouth" he said.

"Go to GW" yelled Parr, the Secret Service agent to the driver Unrue. He was sent to the Emergency room of George Washington University Hospital. The "sirens" were screaming around the Presidential limousine. The police had to clear the way along Connecticut Avenue to 17th street. It was a five block run. The press secretary, a James Brady finding a phone rang the White House and spoke to an aide there called Larry Speakes. "Shots have been fired. Brady's down. I don't know about the President " he said. In fact Brady was lying on the ground in a "pool of blood". Not only had this been noticed by the observers but a secret service agent and a Washington policeman had also been hit!

It was a near miss occasion for the President who had difficulty breathing and needed more blood which the doctors had to intravenously pump into him. The "frothy blood" gushing from his mouth gave rise to a collapsed lung. His pulse couldn't be heard anymore. Thinking he had passed away Parr said a silent prayer for him "Oh, my God, we've lost him."

It was uncertain at the immediate time, whether he would survive. However, it came to pass that the odds against him proved negative, and his hospitalization in the Emergency Room revived his condition. He was not in good shape. The doctors concerns focused on his bleeding for it would appear "he was bleeding to death…." When he eventually came to, his wife Nancy, who was looking over him in hospital, told her upon awaking "Honey, I forgot to duck".

Although he was still just alive, Secretary Haig ordered the State Department to send a message to the government "to which you are accredited". "You will have heard that there was an attempt on the life of President Reagan. His condition is stable… the government in Washington continues to carry out its obligations to its people and its allies."

Secret Service discovered the name of the assassin who as said before was a twenty three year old white man from Colorado named John W Hinkley JR. He had been identified by a Texas Tech student ID card in his wallet. "

The bullet was finally removed back at the hospital which proved the cause of the bleeding. Reagan's condition was hardly good. He had lost a great deal of blood, as much as 8-9 pints which is half the blood in the body. He was dying.

In the midst of the confusion at the White House, the Vice President was prepared to take Office in light of the serious confrontation in front of him and the President's entourage thought of the process it had to take during the interim.

They would have to follow the twenty fifth Amendment process of temporarily replacing the President if a majority agreed he was "incapable of functioning."

Moynihan, who had been around during the time of the other

assassination of the Democratic President, who he worked for applauded Reagan saying something to the effect that the President was making good recovery. He quoted Ernest Hemingway who described courage as "grace under pressure." His comment was forthcoming as he described it;" I do not know that we have seen so great a display. It makes us proud of our President. It is perhaps no time to talk about the Nation, but it is the Nation that nurtured that quality in him, and we are all enhanced by it…we are surely proud of him."

After a long operation, he was out of the surgery room, and by the time he came to, the first thing he wanted to know was about the shooter "why did he do it?" Reagan positively wanted to know the answer here regardless of his condition. The dean of the medical school, a Dr O'Leary said "the President's vital signs were absolutely rock stable through this whole thing…"He was at no time in any serious danger."

The point of the matter was that the President suffered a collapsed lung at the age of seventy, and the drugs administered to him were enough to "dazzle" anyone no matter how brilliant they may be. Besides this, he had lost most of the blood in his body, and blood was being forced into him to save him. However, he made it into the Recovery Room!

The headline news within thirty-six hours hit the streets and they were good reports such as "Reagan in Good Spirit, Making a fast recovery." It was true that he was already working from his hospital bed in spite of the medicine and morphine he had to take to ease the pain.

The man who would have killed him, John W Hinkley, knew Reagan was going to the conference at the Hilton from a copy of the Washington Star. He climbed on board a Greyhound bus. He purchased a ticket to New Haven Connecticut, because he wanted to see the movie star, Jodie Foster, who was a co student at Yale University as well. He wanted to tell her he loved her. He checked in to a hotel in Washington DC and saw from the newspaper the President's schedule for the day. He wrote a letter to Jodie Foster declaring he intended to kill the President to prove his love for her. "I would abandon the idea of getting Reagan in a second, if only I could win your heart," he wrote though he never sent the letter. Apparently, there was no reason apart from disclosing some disturbance of mind from a sick young man whose fantasies about the movie star moved him to the conflict imposed on the President and his cavalcade of secret service agents and police! It is considered a terrible tragedy beginning with the victimization of the President of the United States! The press on the whole upgraded his leadership as one over and above that of "ordinary politicians."

A newspaper political editor wrote; "A new legend has been born. The gunfire that shattered the stillness…created a new hero in Reagan… As long as people remember the hospitalized President joshing his doctors and nurses-and they will remember-no critic will be able to portray Reagan as a cruel or callow or heartless man."Indeed, Reagan was applauded for his courage and determination after a painful surgery to remove the bullet, inches away from his heart…

Another press article put Reagan as "UNIQUE" AND IMPORTANT LEADER OF A MOVEMENT.

"The assassination attempt Monday afternoon left those who share Reagan's dream cold with fear at the futility of going on without Reagan…Far from being the irrelevancy of his caricatures, Reagan is the vital spark that moves his Administration. Even if Bush, with vastly more governmental experience, fully agreed with Reagan's ideological revolutionary goals, he could not match Reagan's ideological commitment. This is what makes the President personally irreplaceable if his Administration is to change the nation…If he had been killed or incapacitated, its radical quality would have been ended."

CHAPTER 28

ANKOR WATT

If the Cambodian case of the 1990's to the 2000's survived history, one can discuss this time as a time, when expense is not mentioned in a conflict where the instruments of torture and terrible cruelty to the Cambodians was demonstrated on a scale by genocidal maniacs. Extermination was the name of their play.

If one remembers the Pol Pot Regime of Cambodia, it is not far removed from the present day program restoring certain nations back on it's feet in a show down of financial wizardry, if this should be considered the description needed. The Khymer Rouge, a notorious gang of genocidal maniacs ruled Cambodia for over a decade until just a year or two ago. I write this in the year 2009! They sent thousands into their prison camps and many more were executed by them at Ankor Watt, the famous architectural splendour of Cambodia once graced and visited by the wife of President Kennedy, Jacqueline. As history restores the jig saw puzzle and assembles the story of the Khymer Rouge, Pol Pot Regime, one cannot dismiss it from the irregularity of human nature's way, reinforcing an ugly path of annihilism to poke fun in the extraordinary genocide committed in the fairest ground in all Cambodia, being Ankor Watt. This is in itself a test of some better intelligence to explain how this came about. Some may simply prefer to look upon this part of the case, as a desecration of the most important city in the whole of this small kingdom without any other explanation to satisfy and resolve such a strange or peculiar problem and threat often reviewed and repeatedly re-enacted like a true phenomena of a sick mind! For better or for worse, it did happen and it did occur every day and every night, to further the terrorism act of the despotic and sadistic regime which rejected the presence and rule of their true Prince Sihanouk, Ruler of the Cambodians in exile. The Cambodians requested him to return time after time, only to be dispelled by the terror and gross annihilism of the Pol Pot, Khymer Rouge regime. They came in from a country bordering between Laos and Cambodia. Government fled and most Cambodians, dancers in Temples, artists, teachers, in fact the best, were assassinated ,their human remains in a pyre built as high as a pyramid to prove the war of genocide in that region. If the Mental Health Act can be blamed, then one could say to some extent, that the true sickness of those who can be blamed in all honesty get away with it, and the author takes the time to exercise commenting and questioning the validation of such a program or the integrity of the psychiatric side who do nothing so far about the claims of illness as demonstrated in Ankor Watt!

If one can have the right to suggest that the war brought wealth and riches to either side, then I myself would seek out the necessary information to prove that the deliberation was done on a mass scale for financial betterment. As far as I know, Ankor Watt will never be the same again, and much of it has been too badly damaged and destroyed from this period of history, that the ruins of Ankor Watt is presently all that is available to the visitor who may be so courageous to go for a visit there as an not so normal "tourist"

CHAPTER 29

THE LAST WAR – FINANCIAL UNCERTAINTY
THE ORGIN OF MONEY

Money has been a part of ordinary day life for at least 2500 years. Herodotus explains how money was invented and coined in Asia Minor. He says how prostitution was the oldest trade for women. "All the young women of Lydia prostitute themselves by which they procure their marriage position…The manners and customs of the Lydians do not essentially vary from those of Greece, except where prostitution is concerned. They are the first people on record who coined gold and silver into money, and traded in retail. "Otherwise, coined money had no value as a guarantee of payment. It was abused until banks and government used these coins as substitutes for money which they promised paying with, and accordingly these promises developed into what we now understand and know to be money. However the abuse system did continue for a while and the uncertainty by the customer as to what they were receiving exactly resulted in some doubt as to their value and what they would be able to buy with them.

In the past 19ᵗʰ century, money became more reliable. The majority of the problem of money management had been resolved as opportunities arose to work for it and even obtain unsecured earnings for small enterprises. By World War 1, money was no longer reliable but an illusion! In life, men view history and over a period of time, we learn how things can only improve. "The history of money gives no support for this optimism."

From the beginning, history tells us that money was coined, and the stamping and minting of pieces of metal is what has been known as money pieces. Otherwise, traditions tells us "cattle, shells, chunks of metal, whisky, and tobacco have been used." Perfume was also bought and sold. Pieces of gold and silver could be put into a purse which was durable and steadfast giving trade to the user proving he could buy and sell with it. This way of holding money is now obsolete and unless one is a collector of old coins, one does not use them anymore. They are a souvenir of the past which reminds us of what was once money. After a time, banks held money and the coins were held there. The first successful and known banks flourished in Roman times, eventually developing in Venice, Florence and Genoa. Banks held power and this power was given to private citizens to be used for making money.

Amsterdam is a city which has many banks connected to the development of financial history in the first banking world. Silver coins became a part of the trade over gold. The weight of each coin measured gave the coins their proper value. This was considered a most reliable way to value the silver pieces. It is said with relative honesty, money does two things. "It ranks with love as man's greatest source of joy. And it ranks with death as his greatest source of anxiety." "Over history, it has oppressed all people. It has been abandoned and could be very unreliable, or reliable and very scarce." It has offered another problem. Money can be both "unreliable and scarce." Amsterdam well known for it's canals, tulips and museums showing old Masters such as Rembrandt, Rubens and Van Dyke, was one of the major cities proponent of what would one day be considered the "hubbub" of central financial business with a legacy of diamonds and diamond merchants. In 1633, this city claimed to be the center of the world in art, and it was in that year Rembrandt moved there from Leyden. The "merchant city" could toast of good taste. Many houses from this period of time still stand and still have "possession of the same family". One merchant, a Jan Six, lived in great style and was the proud owner of Dutch Masters on his walls such as Rembrandt, who became a friend of his, listed in his guest book. Amsterdam was a place of flourishing art and it's " spirit" excelled all others.

Amsterdam was also in essence a "merchant city" which showed tolerance, with its men working there to make money in business, "regardless of race, creed or national origin." Much of this city was settled by Huguenots, Portuguese and Spanish Jews. "Amsterdam did business with most people who wished to do business, including those who wanted to fight the Dutch!"

Like much of past history, even monetary innovation or reform carried seeds of some abuse. An important borrower from the Bank was the Dutch East India Company. The members of this company were often bank personnel resulting in "incestuous, even narcissistic" lending and borrowing. The Franklin National Bank in New York, in the 1970's, the London and County in England, in the same years, lent to business firms, which they not only admired, but trusted as well, "because they were their own." Loans and the creation of money by a bank is only possible if depositors do not come back. The East India Company fell on hard times; they were at war with England and many ships never returned. If they did not come back all at once to claim back their money, or if they suspected that they couldn't get hold of their money, they would return. JF Galbraith says "suspected weakness ensures weakness."

The weakness was discovered and confirmed. The depositors showed up and couldn't be paid. After two centuries of service, the Bank of Amsterdam "was wound up".

CHAPTER 30

JOHN LAW

After Louis X1V's death in 1715, France was going through a bad period and mis-fortune. The French Treasury went bankrupt, and the Regent, the Duc d' Orleans, who happened to be" both intellectually and morally bankrupt" had to find somebody who could save him and his country from an otherwise hopeless situation. This resulted in putting their trust into a rascal who could one day, like a magician perform a magical trick and put everything back in order. The French were desperate to find a resolution to their problem.

The available "rascal" was encountered. He was John Law. Some historians say he was a rascal, while others compare him to a genius, due to his ability to set up an unrivaled bank which brought back confidence and capital back into a bankrupted system. The bank was none other than the Banque Royale which was the bank of the Prince Regent of France. By 1717, John law had organized a nominal company in the West called "the Mississippi Company" from which he established the new bank's success, done so that it held all title to all land north from the Gulf of Mexico to Minnesota and east from the Rockies to the Alleghenies. The trouble was that all this was built on supposition in which the imagined metals were sufficient to claim paper money against secured lands as opposed to silver or gold as deposits. Although on paper, there were maps showing the ruins, they were built on "non-existent metal "in the imagination of their mind. This was the backing of the paper notes of money! However in a short term the Prince Regent was able to resolve his problems and his debts. He found almost immediate success and for a time Paris felt better off. John Law came from a background of finances. His father was a well to do goldsmith from Edinburgh.

Paris trusted him and they flocked around believing colonialization was under way and rushed to buy stocks in the Company of the West.

The stock was booming riches. Law used certain "tricks" to increase the "fiduciary levitation." All flocked around the Rue Quincampoix where the old Paris bourse was located to buy and increase a wager. It is written "the excitement was intense and even violent and the noise was hideous." They tried seeing him or catch a glimpse of him. Some actually went inside and asked him to sell him stocks, including women who "offered themselves to add inducement." The game of recycled paper was a "wonderful time". All thought they were getting rich. The word "millionaire" comes from this time and is a French word.

He was most venerated and the most famous in the land. He was ennobled and made Duc d'Arkansas in 1719. By 1720, he was "Comptroller General of France" – Supreme arbiter of all French finances.

Eventually, people began to doubt the notes. They went to Banque Royale and asked for an exchange in silver and gold, that were still available in Louisiana. Paying off with silver and gold was suspect, and severe steps were taken to say ownership of precious metal except in small quantities was a crime! It was apparent to one and all that the Banque Royale could not pay, that the notes were worthless. Law escaped with his life. Parisians wanted to sing a song that recommended that the paper be used in the most vulgar way possible.

The point to make now is that Law had managed to get the Regent out of a "tight spot" besides which he encouraged colonialization and made France prosperous, at least for a short time. The fact remains that a lot of paper money had been created and used, sending it escalating down into disaster. Had they been used more wisely, Galbraith claims, there might have been some good in them.

CHAPTER 31

WAR ON SUCCESS
STUPIDITY PROBLEMS

"Intelligence is a threat to those who do not possess it" says Galbraith, "and there is a strong case for excluding those who do not possess it". By 1914, rulers and generals had sought a World War 1, and by now one realizes that their class and the social order they came from relied on them to make wars often unnecessarily and without much thought to it or consideration of the cost of it both in lives lost as well as the economy of it. Due to their class, they were the favored class and the "royal reaction" by 1914 favored a "territorial imperative" and the fear it engineered for the sake of mobilizing a somewhat "stupid rule" by the rulers and generals who continued to put their countries into a war process which was by now out of control and without much cause or reason. The Generals of World War 1 were considered completely "brainless "men. As a result, this produced a "negative result" and a "rogue reaction."

Then we learn that Lenin the Russian Revolutionary became the first young student in Russia who tried to plot in an amateurish way, an assassination attempt on Alexander 111.It is written that his Mother appealed for him asking the czar his pardon in St Petersburg, but this was refused because he was unrepentant. The czar eventually met him and admired "his staunch character". Lenin was taught a lesson and his brother was executed by hanging. His looks are famous with a typical revolutionary look of the day; he had long free flowing beard, untidy appearance, a high forehead accentuated by the bald dome above, and a neat moustache… he could have been an accountant in a firm."

While Marx wrote, Lenin acted. Lenin was the "disciple" of Marx, though he never behaved ever as if he was his servant. Very much against Marx's beliefs, Lenin wholeheartedly believed in a successful revolutionary action continuing his belief with his close friends and intellectual allies, all of them disciplined and committed men . The aim was to corporate a body of people rather than a less reliable contentious mass. His target was to unite against the ruling classes in his work as a revolutionary. His belief rang true, when the "working class" parties of Germany and France voted for a war. The birth of the "Social Democrats" was created by the revolutionary worker's party. After this, those committed to the revolution would be called Communists.

Lenin worked for the future of gaining a share of Russian capitalism and participation for the working classes who had often known abuse and ridicule often ignored and without any land. While Marx wrote, Lenin acted upon the understanding that land must be given over to the peasants in order to find a way of creating money by their toil and industry on it. They became "conservative" property owners, thanks to him, until Stalin took over redeeming the land "for the truly Socialist society."

Lenin's efforts to restore the peasants was based on a slogan "peace, bread and land."

CHAPTER 32

JOHN FOSTER DULLES

A religious man, his belief lay with the "doctrine on which to base the Cold War." The Cold War was not about economics but a crusade for moral values – good against bad, right against wrong, religions against dark atheism. It was the defense of faith in the good God for the average neighborly God fearing citizen. They were conceived for belief of oneself and the neighbor.

He was from a small town in Upper New York State. His father was a Presbyterian minister. He had a brother, Allen Walsh Dulles who was his "partner at law" and who would one day be a key player to help him in the time of the Cold War and it's front. He went to Princeton University though his parents wished him to follow in his father's footsteps and become a minister like him. This was not to be. He persuaded his parents to study law, and after a visit to the Hague and Versailles conferences, was much taken and impressed by the work of diplomatic discussions. He worked as a lawyer in a firm called Sullivan and Cromwell, the most prestigious of the great Wall Street firms. His career commenced from this point-.

Most who met him believed in him because of his brilliance. Harold MacMilland said of him…"his speech was slow, but it easily kept pace with his thought." Many thought him a little paranoid in the sense of his drawback to Communists and yet others admired his popularity amongst Soviet Russians. During the Suez Crisis of 1955-56, for instance, he sided with the Soviets against the British, French and Israelis. Dulles was a leader for right against wrong. It has been said that "no power assumed public success." Douglas MacArthur was like this, so also Charles de Gaulle and Winston Churchill. Lenin is compatible to this list. An old Scottish saying goes "where MacCrimson sits is the head of the table". It means, it is better to be MacCrimson then have brilliance of mind, eloquence of speech, or charm of personality. After the Second World War, John Dulles participated with the National Council of Churches. He resumed foreign policy and helped negotiate peace with the Japanese in the Treaty with Japan. Under Eisenhower in 1953, he was appointed Secretary of State. Although not as popular with Democratic Administrators and Kennedy himself, on the grounds probably of "self-righteousness" which he believed was the "moral fruit of simple moral judgment of the Cold War" he was a moral crusader. He was always the religious crusader. He was a crusader of Christian faiths. He was strong on this point though he avoided "brute power" and would have the endorsement of Jesus. The path was set for the liberation for "rolling back the Iron Curtain" had the Hungarian uprising not intervened and it's ugly murder in 1956. He said in a moment of religious thought "Christians are not negative, supine people." They do not exercise "brute power to secure their ends."

On the other hand, the Soviets had a commitment to a world revolution with a "sequence of action" to prove it. In the West however, one could foresee the growing commitment on the grounds of both moral and religious faith, that liberation from Communism was the way for a better future. The fifties proved that Dulles was the man of the time over Eisenhower. Although criticized for his "soft approach to the Soviets" he was verbally ever in agreement with the favored majority such as Dean Acheson, Adlai Stevenson, Averell Harriman or Herbert Lehman. He was involved in a system of intellectuals of government circles (Air Force, Economics, Mathematicians and political science professors) agencies were part of the central Cold War Strategy. It was a time of the CIA it is said, where all intellectual groups were automatically "suspects" . Although friendly at all times with the Soviets, he thought Communists somewhat unscrupulous but upholding always his moral doctrine for Christian principles held as a weapon of "independent force."

CHAPTER 33

VIETNAM

JK Galbraith asks if the Vietnam War was also a part of a "moral crusade?" Was it a crusade dispatched to the Holy Land to redeem Sodom or Gomorrah, the saving of South Vietnam with US involvement to enforce an anti Communist way American-style for a "key" into South East Asia? The stake for America was big enough to ask often enough, why their commitment was endured in a near suicidal fight for liberty and freedom in an eventual free South East Asia. Years of fighting, was the irreversible test. The Vietnam War years destroyed America's stamina and moral view point of testing out their control over South East Asia in the worst fight against Communism. They regarded at that time that South East Asia was being conspired on by the worst conspiracy of all being the forces of Communism. It was a revenge scorning freedom and liberation of rights of man opposing indoctrination of principles defying national good and the democracy of any given Christian society. Christian society gives human understanding and does a lot to live in harmony with each other as a humanitarian state of any Christian who believes in such a society. Russia lived in "Manchukuo," China at this time. Dulles referred to "atheistic Communism" a state of dark Middle Ages and living in a non Christian, ungodly limbo. It was the time for many who upheld anti-Christ principles to pave a disorder and practice extermination of a world for it. Suffering is conspiratorial and multi-faced, prodding the weakness of non-believers of Communism. This automatically thrust the process into a Cold War which engaged a crusade led by Dulles to liberate the world of atheistic Communism, for a purpose controlled by Divine Will.

The Vietnam War never stopped by 1965. President Richard Nixon continued this war and at the same time took steps to visit the Chinese in China, and Soviets in the Soviet Union. He was the President who confirmed the policy of "détente" meaning obscured when translated from the French. By 1976, President Ford dropped this word to replace it for an emphasis on "peace." It was a significant step to change it all against "irreconcilable conflicts" of one side seeking the destruction of the other side, at whatever cost it took. They encountered old ideas again. "The arms race now became the trap."

CHAPTER 34

THE TRAP

The talk was all about "the bomb". By 1945 talks took place between Stalin and Truman at Potsdam. They discussed the atom bombs. This did not successfully "defuse" the main worry about them. By this stage, it had become a source of commerce in the market place and there was certain competition in the nuclear arms race, most unfortunately. They wanted to develop the new weapons as it had become "the new order of the day" and there was quite a lot of interest in them which resulted in the original talks ending in a stale mate position.

At Cape Cod, Massachusetts, at Woods Hole, the talk was of "tryouts of nuclear submarines". They wanted to experiment on nuclear missiles that could be fired from a submarine which when underwater and out of sight and undetected could devastate a target of up to 3000 miles away. They were talking of the famous Polaris. This belonged as part of the arms race for the Soviets who were contemplating creating one for themselves. This contest proves that both the Soviets and the Imperialists Americans were both guilty. Both sides must ultimately defend itself from the other.

One never understands the words "cost-effectiveness" when speaking of arms for defense. It is equal says JK Galbraith to expenditures for "civilians in health, housing, mass transport, low taxes to more private consumption." In years to come the economic question would be put under pressure to "limit arms not against it," he says. The present arms race entrapment is not a case of survival. It must be better confronted and has already been discussed in previous chapters.

What is leadership?

The great leaders of the world have one common trait. "It is to confront the major anxieties of their people." This is called "essence of leadership." The 1932 Great Depression gave proof that President Hoover, a most distinguished and well educated man and not at all foolish, hardly knew how to confront this time and it's economic catastrophe. For instance, he told everyone "the slump is over" when clearly it never was. He pushed harder without knowing it for economic recovery and better financial health. The 1929 Crash of Wall Street led up to the years of terrible Depression both in the US and in Europe. People suddenly lost their money. It is said of this time that it is the" fall of money and nothing else is lost but money" that we are reminded of Dulles once more, who never lost sight of God and better morals and better beliefs than Communism to live by. But the worst catastrophe may have fallen on most of the world in 2009, when a type of 1929 Crash invalidated democracy by the eventual murders in the world and a Depression reigned supreme as banks ran out of loans and money to better support the people .In Japan, the financial losses have been told of late, and maybe the best comparison is to read all over again the Dickins story "A Tale of Two Cities." If Wall Street has a "deus ex machine" it did not applaud the goings on of their Enrons or their Madoffs. At a time before the Wall Street Crash, many wanted to be rich quick. Their greed became a part of their lunacy. This caused the break up and the Crash. It was a lesson for all to learn. They took on "an escape from reality" that did carry an authority greater than the Government. One remembers too how it was thought "unwise to be sane at a time when sanity exposed one to "ridicule, persecution, condemnation for spoiling a game, or the threat of severe political retribution." There is no sense in talking about customers who upon hearing of their complete loss of money or bankruptcy, jumped out of high buildings to perish lying dead in the street. If this happened in 1929, how could we have anticipated the worst recession ever in time by a credit crunch which has devoured the money in a lunatic frenzy. It is added that during the Wall Street Crash, "nobody led the investors to the slaughter". How it changed Japan and the worst followed, worse than 9/11! It has already been said that when there has been fall of money, it is a time of great tragedy. Practically, no way in terms of diplomacy or world financial law, as well as international law and all codes put together by Napoleon himself years before can fix an insane greed and loss of reason for material success and money. The wonder is that in the U.S. and most other countries in the world who knew they would never want to confront another Crash like this again, could tell us now that for a certainty 1929 burned itself out. Eventually on a world stage, we discover there were certain people whose natural talents and abilities earned them vast fortunes. Take for instance Michael Jackson pop star, or the case of Prince Henri, of France.

I once saw a TV program about Prince Henri, of France otherwise known as le Comte de Paris, and Michael Jackson, pop star. The first case deals with one of the wealthiest landlords in France who owned the best chateaux and sold them for an enormous amount of money. He then went on to selling his assets stored in the chateaux. He was married to a Princess who was his wife, and together they produced nine children. He sold his establishments for them, and after the sales, put his proceeds into a Swiss Bank Account, at the same time leaving his wife of many years, and Mother to his nine heirs, to live in an elegant but very small house outside Paris with his maid who served in one of his former homes, now sold. One evening, the President of France came to have dinner with them. He kissed Prince Henri on the cheek - a custom in France. After dinner, Francois Mitterand left, and after a little time, Prince Henri discovered losses of much of his invested wealth in the accounts held for his children in Switzerland. He was probably considered one of the wealthiest men of France before the losses, incurred after the dinner with the French President. Later on, some of his children died or were left dis-inherited. I believe only two survived the tests and became the heirs to the fortune that remained after the time of Francois Mitterrand. The case is a little about succession rights being interfered with greatly to have the devastating effect it did have at the end where the heirs were concerned. Some lost it all and others remained employed to gain what remained after the death of their venerated father.

In the case of Michael Jackson , he was shown as a singular bachelor, alone a lot of the time in a hotel room, sitting there with a bottle of vodka at hand watching TV and drinking his best drink. He ate little and seems to have suffered from a hospital who organized him, legalized by the sight of ambulances for instance. They used to pick him up from the airport, and one guesses he had to serve them and possibly pay them. He had stopped being met by then by screaming fans and notable agents wishing to have press conferences with him. The star it seems faced certain bias on his success and fortune as the formidable and kindly young man to others, his gentle goodness and personality questioned. His vast fortune and success, that could have been better enjoyed seems to have ended him in court rooms with parents seeking justice from him as he was motioned as a pedophile and child molester. In a press conference I saw him at, in a hotel in Montreux Switzerland, he said that he knew the faces of danger and realized he could die at any moment. He was philosophical about this, and never allowed this to overwhelm his life or draw the fear it was intended to do. If he died, this year, in July 2009, in the USA, they wanted to have better information concerning his very sudden death, and to interrogate his GP and close friend. Some suspect foul play. The case was soon resolved. The war against his personal wealth was challenged by couples accusing him of molestation. They were settled and soon the case came to an end. Although a candidate of great wealth, his apparent death may realize a greater loss for many who loved and knew him. I think many will remember the songs he wrote and sang.If any lessons can be worked out about the financial problems to be resolved, one must look back to see better what not to do and leave the rest to be improved upon.

One notices that taxation cannot equalize all races and nations to live by the creed of minimizing one's outgoings per couple. One child per couple can earn enough to pay for working or everything as well as the taxes. I do not yet know if this is not an awful life of hum drum mediocrity offered to each couple. The change has occurred however and it would be a person lacking realism to suggest it can all go back to the way it was, like a snap of the finger. Many conflicts are still in store and many more civil disputes will erupt no doubt as the fights go on about their "jealousy, love and hate…as time goes by". Here one sees that it is not for financial worth, but a backing for a race horse track which is not quite the same business as writing a romantic novel about a love affair, get it published and paid for it! This is my very simple point in the contest if there is one at all.

Rebirth and rebuilding of any nation will probably insist on low nuclear mileage meaning a request to forget the nuclear bombs as a priority. If bombs were to be more important than housing, transport, schools, churches , construction and the building of dams for water for power, than we would all agree that it is a self destruct approach which can only defeat oneself and hold the rest of the world to ransom! Commerce and fair trade with other nations must be in line with most dealers of any craft and trade essential to any and all nations. We must avoid the nuclear and commit one and all to keep the peace in regions most afflicted by war. We must evade the nuclear holocaust and as JF Galbraith says in his experience and knowledge of the diplomatic world and author of "The Age of Uncertainty" that a "commitment to this reality is now the supreme test of our politics. None should accept the easy evasion that the decision is not ours. …The Russians are no… more inclined to a death wish than we. We must believe, for it is true that they are as willing as we are to commit themselves to this reality, to the existence of this threat to all life and to its elimination."

"That indeed is the highest purpose of politics in both countries, one…that transcends the differences in economic or political systems. For after the first exchange of missiles, the ashes of Communism and the ashes of Capitalism will be indistinguishable. Not even the most passionate ideologues will be able to speak of the difference, for he too will be dead. In an age when so much is uncertain, there is one certainty: This truth we must confront."

The best must be to do one thing at a time to get the full success of all the successes put together. It must be the point in time to share peace with each other more than anything else. This must pave the financial route much better and give it no opposition for growth and stability depend on it. If this should be opposed, we will indeed be forced to live a most oppressive life with little scope for a brighter and better off tomorrow.

Although democracy can be restored, the obstacles ahead for the eventual course to peace and freedom is the sodomy and prostitution and terror as the course to wreck havoc on an already frail world just recovering from a global credit crunch and financial recession including bankruptcies.

The word must be for peace and security to bring back stability. If a road could promise fulfillment of this and confidence brought back in the economy, it is obvious the world can resume normality or as near to it as possible. The situation has yet to be seen and only another atomic war could beset the hopes of most people around the world,working for a better established and settled order.

Democracy must be restored and where there is a will there must be a way to regain that peace fought so hard for, in the name of freedom.

Author

Tokiko Matsudaira

Chiswick, London,

England

re-vised and re-edited August 2010

This cycle if repeatedly administered by enforced brutality against innocence, will pave a terrible path to further conflicts and possible terror wars. How to combat any insurgencies like this can only be an act of War eventually. The talk now is of victory of certain nations to declare themselves nuclear states ready to fight at any moment. The fight could be a way of re-living a defense strategy against increasing terror alerts and mad devastations of ruthless murder for financial robbery and conquest of money. The wanton expression of any terror war could so openly declare itself in such a manner. It could erupt anywhere in the world.

It was all for the Conquistadores once upon a time. They say the same thing except in a different language speaking often of being conquerors, for the unspoken words following power struggles. They seek to conquer for wealth, be it a gold mine, a diamond mine or a bank full of bonds, securities and money. Like an old world, living once in splendor and wealth as conquerors of world domains, the history repeated uses different language, different clothing and different manners. The Empire seekers wish to be restored of the system of more revenues and financial well being as before. Then the partiality that only a few women will exist in the world demanded by men for the bed, there can be no more trouble or competition from other women whose change would substantiate against any claims that they were ever women at all, having changed into flowers, as a method imposed on a calendar by a conspiracy formed by one government or the other to help the once over-looked "queer". The erosion of normal men or women is a great devastation for most decent living human beings. The drugs the women take speaks for their attitude and demands, sympathized with or not, a case of wonderful returns for a little "rien du tout!" As farcical as it sounds, the essence is there of what could transpire into the reality of all condemned by those worshipped as government gods. The cycle could be re-set. The rest remains to be seen. The foregone conclusion is not useful but may be backed by communists. They no longer stoop to conquer. This difference makes them the newly established order amongst some who believe in them as the new founders of the recycle, a path to leave most behind.In spite of all the talk of cut backs in a time of financial recovery, the hypocrisy lies in the fact that much more money is given away for the few to live the lives of the very wealthy, when they never worked for it but which sadly is invested in them for the inconvenience caused on many different communities and to upset the financial world at large as well. We can only wait to see what can or will be the future if there will be one to speak of at all.

I do not know at this point how personal it is to myself, my family or friends, but I could guess there is some grain of truth in the surmised reality about the futures. Wasn't it as said before, never a game of "lambs being led to the slaughter" but a game of futures where we are axed down to provide another with our personal or professional futures? It sounds an incredible joke to say they ask us to die for them.

The nuclear may be a part of the problem for nobody can fight a nuclear bomb threat. It is doubtless a bad choice but may be a necessary one under the circumstances.

As peace is restored in one area of the world, the relativity is that unrest and revolt topple another. Is this a see-saw effect all over again?

Whatever achievement was gained in Iceland between Reagan and Gorbachev, it is not without reason that the policy was achieved because globally, the world was at peace. Nowadays, too many new wars and conficts have openly availed terrorists to thug on most for a search and want of being socially accepted and no longer a part of a classless society but from a better class. This corruption has so far gone hand in hand with financial demands and privileges not given before. After the 9/11 terrorism attack on the Twin Towers in New York City, the following years proved the Arabs offer of money in to the big banks helping the U.S. Government at a time when they needed financial reserves the most shed new light on a change of circumstances both sides. The Saudis proved they too could be friends to the Americans at a time when the US federal reserve was most in need opening the doors of America to them which was the welcome position for both Arabs and Americans alike, though not the committed feeling amongst the general population.

Nuclear arms and preparations for it, are an over-throw of all actions of war. I think this book cannot foresee the future but has observed until 2010, what has been the on-going process in the world betrayed by so much war and it's propaganda. It can only remain to be seen what history will enfold in later years after this book.

ABOUT THE AUTHOR

Tokiko "Toki" Matsudaira was born in August 1944, in Tokyo, Japan at the Red Cross Hospital. At age six, she was sent to the Unites States, where she was brought up and educated in the Sacred Heart School in upper New York state.

Cost of Freedom, which was much inspired by Glen Miller's music, was conceived from the idea of aircraft and air force, and delivered this book as a theme starting with World War II kamikaze pilots.

The historical outlook of World War II is expanded and developed as a continuation of arguments for or against nuclear arms that Japanese presidents and American presidents have held. Their perspectives of the world where nuclear war games could develop is discussed.

In 1969, she moved from Tokyo to London, England, where she had worked in various art galleries. She is divorced and has two children.

www.ingramcontent.com/pod-product-compliance
Lightning Source LLC
Chambersburg PA
CBHW040535170726
48295CB00012B/474